MADE MEN III

CHLOE

SARAH BRIANNE

YOUNG INK PRESS

Young Ink Press Publication
YoungInkPress.com

Connect with Sarah:
AuthorSarahBrianne@gmail.com
www.facebook.com/AuthorSarahBrianne
@AuthorSarahBri

CHLOE

THE DEMON HAD COME TO GET HER

PRESENT TIME

Chloe *stared at the blank,* white wall in front of her bed, still clutching the jacket Amo had draped carefully across her shoulders earlier that night. Something about his jacket was keeping the demons at bay. Maybe it was the fact that it smelled like him, or maybe it was the warmth making her feel as if his arms were wrapped—

Crack!

The sound of broken bones greeted her ears as a baseball bat slammed down on a limp body, the image flashing on the wall in front of her for a split second.

Coming back to reality, she almost forgot where her thoughts were heading. If she hadn't inhaled Amo's masculine scent coming from the expensive fabric, then that was where her mind would have gone. She started to think the jacket might have been soothing her, but she hadn't experienced that feeling in a long time. The only reason she believed it was because her thoughts should be consumed right now by her horrors, making her watch the replay of tonight's—

Snap!

Another flash of the bat making contact with the man's leg, the man who lay practically lifeless on the floor, before the wall turned blank again.

She ran her thumb over the fabric, not understanding why her body wouldn't stay motionless like the million times it had before when her nightmares had played in front of her eyes.

Gliding her thumb over the soft fabric again, she came to the conclusion that it felt as expensive as it—

An evil pair of blue-green eyes stared back at her from the white wall, making her blood run cold. She watched him grip the neck of the bat with a force so intense she was positive it was going to shatter before the bat was brought down for its final time.

Crunch!

Amo's jacket was no longer going to bring her out of her nightmarish dream.

The demon had come to get her.

GOING BACK IN TIME

FOUR YEARS EARLIER

The stinging pain on her face and her sore body woke her, making her want to scream, but her throat was too dry. Not only did the room feel unfamiliar to her, but the sterile smell, as well. She couldn't recall anything nor figure out where in the world she was, which made her feel as if she were heavily drugged.

As she groggily tried to open her eyes, she saw everything in a blur. Then a figure moved into the space over her.

"Chloe," a male said before he laid his hand over her arm.

The moment his masculine hand touched her skin, memories flooded her mind of the horrific crimes she had just endured, like she was going back in time to endure it all again.

She tried desperately to scream, but it sounded weak, coming out as a hoarse whisper.

When the pressure from the hand on her slightly increased, she began to kick and hit uncontrollably, unsure if she could survive the brutality she had just experienced once more.

"It's me, your father. Chloe, you're safe now," her father kept repeating quietly, trying to keep her calm.

All she could think about was the hand on her arm, as if she were still experiencing the torturous touch from before.

Only wanting it to stop, she was finally able to scream, "Let go of me!"

Her father only held her down harder, using both hands.

"Shh! You are safe . . . in the hospital," he began, trying everything he could to keep her from drawing attention to the room.

Hot tears spilled down her cheeks before the sound of shuffling feet echoed throughout the room, and even more hands began to hold her down.

"Please, I can't take anymore!" she cried.

"She's having a panic attack. Give her something!" her father quickly spit out before Chloe could say another word.

Feeling a slight sting in her arm, Chloe started to lose the fight against them. Unfortunately, as her body became numb, her mind didn't. She still felt her torturer's hands on her instead of the people in this room.

Looking past the nurses, she stared at the blank, white wall through the blur of her tears.

Please, I don't want to be touched anymore.

"S-Stop!" Chloe choked out for what felt like the hundredth time as hands held her down once more.

The prick of the needle into her sore skin felt like nothing compared to the hands that gripped her. Her cheeks burned as tears fell, bringing her to the realization that she must have been crying in her sleep as she was never even awake for a full five minutes before they knocked her out again.

As the drugs took over her body, her last thought was to wish they understood.

The nurses, along with her father, thought she was screaming for them to stop drugging her, but she was just screaming for them to pull their hands off her body.

The fuzziness in her brain started to ease as she woke. Chloe regained consciousness once more, having no idea how long she had been at the hospital or how many times she had woken up, only for it to end in screams and pain. This time, she lay unmoving, afraid to even open her eyes.

The pain on her face had her wanting to relieve it.

Don't move.

The memories of the man …

Don't cry.

Chloe had to fight her instincts and to think smart about how to keep them from continuing to drug her. *Otherwise, there will be nothing left of me . . . if there is anything left.*

Even with her eyes closed, she could feel a presence in the room, and considering her father had been there every time she had awakened, it was safe to say he was that presence. She wasn't even sure if he had ever left the room, but the question was, why?

Her father had wanted to talk, but the moment she'd become hysterical, he wouldn't even give her a chance to cry it out, making her feel as if she were crazy.

Why?

Hearing a movement come from the far corner of the hospital room, she knew he was awake, so she decided to take the distance between them to her advantage.

Chloe didn't open her eyes as she began to open her mouth, afraid if she did, her hysteria would take over, and the cruel cycle would start again.

"I-I don't like to be touched anymore," she whispered as best she could.

She heard what sounded like her father starting to get up.

A face flashed in her mind as she felt invisible hands wrap around her throat.

"No!" Her eyes shot open to reveal the dim hospital room. Chloe took a deep breath, trying to keep her voice even, to remain calm. "Don't come closer . . . please."

After a moment, her father sat back in his chair.

The room was eerily quiet. She didn't understand why he wasn't asking her questions, wondering what had happened or, more importantly, who had done this to her.

Does Dad already know? Is the man locked up forever?

She figured she would start with that first.

"You know what happened to me, don't you?"

The look on his worn out face gave her the answer.

Her father held up his hands and slowly stood. "I'm not going to touch you. I just want to come closer. Is that all right?"

Trying her best to stay strong, she nodded her head, holding her breath as he slowly walked toward her. She only slightly relaxed as he stood by the bed, making no attempts to touch her.

He looked down upon her, taking in this new sight of his daughter.

When her silent questions still went unanswered, she forced herself to whisper the words, "Did you catch him?"

A bushy eyebrow rose as he stared at her blankly. "Catch who?"

Shocked, Chloe blinked a few times, wondering if she were in a dream before the stinging on her face told her it wasn't.

"Who did this to me?" she choked out.

"Chloe, you were in a car accident." It sounded as if it were rehearsed.

"There was no car—"

"You were in a car wreck; that's all you know." His voice was calm and collected.

Chloe began shaking her head violently, her eyes brimming with tears. "No, I wasn't. He hurt—"

"You were in a car wreck. No one hurt you."

"N-no!" she screamed as her cheeks started to burn again from the tears.

"You were in a car wreck; that's all you know. You were in a car wreck. No one hurt you." He was beginning to sound hypnotic.

Not only her head, but her body began to violently shake. "NO! NO! NO!"

This time, a lone nurse came in the room with a needle, closing the door behind her.

Her father stepped forward, holding her down, as Chloe tried to scream as loudly as her throat allowed, fighting off their hands as much as she could before the needle pricked her skin in the sore spot of her arm.

He spoke over her with the same, melodic sound in his voice. "You were in a car wreck; that's all you know. You were in a car wreck. No one hurt you ..."

DOES THE SIGHT OF HER JUST SICKEN YOU?

Sitting up in the hospital bed, she hadn't moved, hadn't spoken. She merely sat there, doing the same thing for hours: staring. The white wall in front of her was the only thing she stared at. It showed her past, her nightmares.

I was in a car wreck.

Hearing the click of kitten heels getting closer and closer to the door didn't bring her out of her trance.

A woman with short black hair and dressed in business attire entered the room. Not a hair on her head was out of place, and the pearls wrapped around her neck perfectly gleamed. It was the first time she had seen Chloe since the "accident," so she took a few moments to look her over.

"It's a shame they——I mean, she got her face marked. I think we could use it to our advantage and turn this situation into something better." Her beady eyes travelled down. "However, I think she should keep her arms covered; we don't want people to feel too sorry for us."

That's all I know.

Turning, she walked toward Chloe's father, who was staring out the window.

"Why don't you go home and get some rest, Maxwell? You look tired. I'll go back to the office and keep taking care of everything. Let the nurses do their job."

Maxwell didn't even turn to look at her. "Did you ever love our daughter, or does the sight of her just sicken you?"

"We've talked about this." Chloe's mother sighed.

Turning his head, he looked at her with disgust. "How does the sight of her look to you now?"

I was in a car wreck.

"Please don't bring this up here in front of her."

"What do you see in her, Elaine? Your sister or the pride you lost in your womanhood when you found out you couldn't have a child naturally?"

"Yeah, well, I guess you picked the wrong sister," Elaine huffed.

Maxwell resumed staring out the window. "I know I did."

Elaine stormed off toward the door. "I would tell you to leave me for her, but you can thank your daughter for killing her."

The snap of the door closing had him looking away from the window to Chloe.

A single tear had slid down her cheek.

"Don't listen to her." He stood, going to her bedside and opening a medicine bottle.

No one hurt me.

He placed a little, white pill in the dip of a spoon and held it to her mouth. "This will make it all better."

Getting discharged should have made her happy, but those little, white pills the doctor had prescribed her wouldn't let her feel much of anything. They weren't making her a vegetable, unable to move, but they were making her feel hollow, like a shell.

"Go get yourself cleaned up. I can still smell hospital all over you," her mother spewed as she scrunched up her nose in distaste.

Chloe headed toward the bathroom, turning the light on and closing the door behind her. She hadn't realized it until now, but she had been avoiding mirrors for this exact moment in time.

The high dose of medication might make her unable to feel, but the bile running up her throat was telling her she should be feeling something.

The right side of her face was still swollen with a slash marking her face from about two inches above her eyebrow all the way down to a now very hollow cheek. The other one was about an inch above and below the right side of her mouth. The marks were fresh and grotesque, flaming a bright red with dried up blood that faded out to red, pink, and rosy on her skin.

Chloe moved her gaze down as she slowly removed the rest of her clothes. She had been so concerned with the pain in her face at the hospital she didn't even noticed her arms shared their own markings.

I was in a car wreck; that's all I know. I was in a car wreck. No one hurt me.

"I don't hear the water running." Her mother swung open the door to reveal Chloe looking at herself with tears in her eyes. Immediately, she stepped into the bathroom, closing the door and going straight to the bathtub to run the water. "Get in."

When Chloe didn't move and just continued to stare at herself in shock, her mother raised her voice. "Chloe. Get. In."

Chloe's glazed eyes moved to look at her mother's in the mirror. "I can clean myself." It had been years since her mother had bathed her. Even though her brain was hazy, she could remember how rough she had been bathed, making washcloths feel like Brillo pads. As soon as she had been able take showers, she had. However, that was before her "accident," back when she could be touched.

"Then do it without getting your stiches wet."

Quickly, she got into the freezing tub. Picking up the washcloth, she held it under the water to give herself a sponge bath.

"You're getting them wet ..." Elaine advised harshly.

She tried to be more careful, but by this point, her vision was too blurry from tears.

"Give it to me." Snatching away the washcloth, her mother got on the floor to reach into the tub.

Chloe started crying, afraid of the moment when her mother's skin would touch hers.

"I can do it!"

"Clearly, you are incapable." Elaine started scrubbing her back, pushing Chloe forward.

"Please! I can do it!" She tried avoiding her touch to no avail. The harder she tried, the harder her mother scrubbed her skin raw. No amount of tears, fighting, or pleading saved her. Much like when she had been kidnapped, it only made her captor relish in her discomfort.

It was far worse than she remembered, but that might just be because any touch was now unwelcome for Chloe.

Looking at her mother as she scrubbed furiously, in her place now stood the man who would forever haunt not only her nightmares but reality.

HOW DOES THE SIGHT OF
HER LOOK TO YOU NOW?

Sleep no longer came for Chloe because sleep was a dangerous thing. Here, awake in her bedroom, alone, staring at the white wall, her kidnapping played before her eyes. It was as if she were watching a movie.

Sure, it scared the shit out of her, but it was better than the alternative.

Here, asleep in her bedroom, alone, with her eyes closed, her kidnapping didn't play on the movie screen. It happened to her all over again.

She could feel hands wrapping around her neck ...

The blade piercing my skin ...

That was what really scared the shit out of her.

Chloe shook her tired head. *No one hurt me.*

It had been a while since her last dose of medication, and her mind didn't seem as fuzzy or numb. Maybe it wasn't a terrible nightmare that kept haunting her, but maybe it was real.

Hours passed as she sat in her misery, contemplating what was real or a dream. Finally, when she heard the footsteps come to the door, she knew she would be rescued from her thoughts, or any thoughts for that matter.

The smell that greeted her nose as her father entered the room had her wrinkling it up. She watched him stumble to her bed, almost falling over several times in the short distance.

"Dad, a-are you all right?"

His words came out harsh and slurred. "Yes-s-s. Why the f-f-fuck wouldn't I be?"

Chloe's heart rate started to rise from the sight of her father drunk, never having seen it before.

She sat quietly and patiently, waiting for him to quit fumbling to get the prescription bottle open.

"You-u-u open it-t." He threw the bottle on the bed.

Grabbing up the bottle, she tried her best not to shake as she opened it and spilled out one of the little, white pills. Closing the bottle, she then quickly placed it on her nightstand, too afraid to hand the bottle to him and risk him touching her.

Maxwell snatched the bottle up forcefully, causing a huge rattling sound to fill the room before he stumbled out the way he had come in.

She sat in shock, gazing at the now closed door, hoping to never see her father come through her door like that again.

Something about him seemed … *Violent, just like him …*

Chloe opened her hand, revealing the little, white pill that sat perfectly in the middle of her palm. Swiftly, she popped the pill into her mouth before swallowing, hoping it would work quickly.

"I was in a car wreck; that's all I know. I was in a car wreck. No one hurt me."

It wasn't long before her father's medicine visits to her room were few and far between. Each time he came in, he was ruder and more drunk than the last visit. Chloe had to learn to deal with the pain on her own as she was slowly weaned off the pills. She didn't know what she dreaded more: a train full of emotions hitting her when the medicine had run its course or her father walking through the door again. It was a flip of a coin which one was worse. They both gave her nightmares.

Something about her was broken, and those pills weren't putting her back together. Instead, they just acted like a Band-Aid, a temporary fix not to feel the emotions that were killing her. The Band-Aid wasn't healing her; it was causing her to rot from the inside out. Deep down, she knew this. She could feel it the moment her last dosage wore off, and that was when she made a decision.

The turning of the doorknob had Chloe jumping up in bed.

Maxwell entered the room in a jumbled mess, reeking of alcohol. Coming over, he practically threw the medicine bottle at her.

Chloe kept her head down as she said, "I-I d-don't want them a-anymore."

"Ex … cu-u-use me?"

Swallowing down the bile that rose in her throat, she said it again. "I d-don't want them anymore."

He stared at her a minute before he responded, "Then … if you don't need them-m anymore, your ass-s-s can go back to s-s-school."

She gasped, finally raising her head to look at him. "P-Please don't make me go back!"

"Yes …"

"No!" She couldn't help crying.

Maxwell pointed his finger right in her face, frightening her into thinking he was going to grab her. "Don't you ever … speak to me that way again lit-t-tle girl." He snatched up the medicine bottle forcefully off the bed. "Now you're fucking going to s-s-school tomorrow. You were just in a damn wreck …, rem-m-member?"

Chloe didn't even hear the door close behind him. She sat there all night, holding herself tightly.

Her father used to be her only source of love and trust. Now he scared the daylights out of her. After her "accident," it was evident she wasn't the only person who had changed.

Now, if her home life wasn't fucked up enough, she had to go back to the outside world. Not only had she not left the house, but she hadn't even left her bedroom. Now she was going to be thrown right back into high school like nothing had even happened.

When morning came, Chloe headed to her bathroom. One look at herself in the mirror and she knew exactly how the kids at school were going to treat her.

Does the sight of her just sicken you?

She remembered how she had used to look just a short time ago. She used to think of herself as pretty.

How does the sight of her look to you now?

Now all she could see was the ugliness that had touched her.

THE ONE WORD THAT WOULD FOLLOW HER FOREVER: "FREAK"

Elaine had dropped her off at school, not an ounce of sympathy in her eyes as she shooed Chloe out of the car so that she would not be late for work. There wasn't a point in pleading not to walk in those front doors with her. She preferred the jungle of Legacy Prep High over being in the car with her, anyway.

As Chloe walked to the front doors of the school, it was a lot for a fourteen-year-old to handle, especially considering what she had gone through since the last time she had walked through those doors. The last time she had passed that doorframe, she not only had looked like a different person, but she had been a different person. The person she was now was unrecognizable.

Maybe it won't be so bad.

Swallowing hard and finally mustering up the courage to open the door, she passed through the entrance. She hoped her new markings would just gain some sort of sympathy, enough to just be left alone. That was all she asked for.

Pulling the sleeves down on her black sweater to cover the tops of her hands, she started walking down the hall. Her heart stopped instantaneously as a wave of silence slowly traveled down the hall. What was once a noisy, shuffling of feet and smashing lockers accompanied by loud gossip and chatter had now become so quiet you could hear a pin drop.

She had known she would be stared at. *Let them get it out of their system. Then it will all be over.*

She had to remind herself to put one step in front of the other and focus on reaching the classroom door as the whispering started in another wave down the hall. Regardless, Chloe couldn't make out anything that was said ... until she heard it—the one word that would follow her forever: "freak."

Chloe hung her head to the ground, letting her long, black, silky hair sweep across her face to cover her scars and shame.

The chuckling from the loudly voiced word began to travel down the hall. She knew who had said it. The certain blonde had just signed Chloe's death sentence. It was a joke for her to think it would all be over soon, the remains of the once very naive little girl.

It felt like an eternity before she reached her classroom where she carefully took a seat in the back. She held her head down as the students filed in, whispering the moment they saw her. Chloe even continued to hold her head down as class started. It wasn't until she heard the classroom door squeak open and complete silence fill the room that she looked up.

Instantly, her heart stopped as she watched a short-haired, strawberry-blonde girl come through the room, taking her seat at the front.

"Did you have a good vacation, Ms. Buchanan?" The teacher raised her brow as she looked down at the tardy girl.

There was some snide giggling among the room before the girl replied, "Sure."

Chloe had to look away from the girl, glancing down at her lap to see that she had been wringing her hands. She had forgotten what had happened the last day she had come to school. She had forgotten what had happened to that poor girl.

What they did to her . . .

Applying more pressure to her hands as she wrung them, she began to hate herself for forgetting. Even after all she had been through, she should have at least thought about her once.

Thought about what I did to her . . .

Staring at her white desk, the memory began to play in front of her . . .

Chloe stared in shock as the group all took turns beating the helpless girl on the ground. She didn't have a clue of what to do as the ring leaders, who happened to be twins, Sebastian and Cassandra, were already doubting her intentions. They were constantly clocking her, seeing how she was reacting and if she was going to run. She had told herself to run for help the moment they had started dragging the girl down the hallway to the outside of the school, but one of them had caught on and grabbed her arm, making her follow along.

If she ran now, there was no doubt they would catch her and give her the same fate as the girl on the ground. Right now, the only chance she had to help her was to watch and wait until they left, and she could get her some help. Otherwise, no one would have a clue she was behind the school, lying there, left helpless.

Looking down at the now bloody girl, bile started travelling up her throat. She wasn't sure how much longer she could watch without giving herself away.

Relief flooded her when they all had taken their turns and went to head back. She wanted to get her help as fast as possible.

"Wait."

However, Sebastian's voice stopped them all in their tracks.

"You didn't get your turn, Chloe."

Swallowing hard, she thought as fast as she could. "That's okay; we're missing lunch, and I'm hun——"

Sebastian shoved her closer to the body on the ground. "Kick her, then, and we can go."

Looking down at her, Chloe's heart started to break.

"She looks like she's had enough."

"You better fucking kick her."

Sebastian and the rest of them all stepped closer to her, making the threat clear.

Taking a few steps closer, she wanted to break down and cry for the girl, cry and scream until someone came to rescue her. There was no way she could kick her.

"Kick me. It doesn't hurt anymore," The bloody girl mouthed quietly for only her to witness.

Feeling the others closing in on her, Chloe closed her eyes and reared her foot back, kicking her in the ribs with enough force to keep them happy, though not hard enough to inflict much more pain on the girl.

"Let's get out of here. The bitch got the message. Good job, Chloe."

They all started to head back once again, but Chloe couldn't move. She had been so disgusted with herself the moment she had done it, but she couldn't figure out another way to get the girl some help in the end.

Staring down at her, she saw the girl staring back with pleading eyes. Chloe could see her begging for her to leave with them, to not continue to arise suspicion. She didn't understand why the girl cared if she got beaten up or not. She shouldn't care, not after what the group she hung around had done to her, and this hadn't even been the first offence.

The strong-willed girl kept pleading, and with the group watching her every move, she turned to leave with them.

She looked down at the ground as she walked away, wanting to cry. I'm so sorry, Elle …

Chloe quickly wiped the tear that had fallen down on her fresh scar.
I deserved what he did to me.

THE WORDS THAT WOULD FOREVER BE INGRAINED IN HER SOUL

Elle was one of the first ones to sit down with her food in the cafeteria. She hadn't waited behind in math class to finish her problem and get the shit beaten out of her when the hallways were deserted. It was also taco day for the main line, which meant the other line of chicken patties and hamburgers was nonexistent, and she had chosen that option.

It was her first day back since the beating, and she was keeping to herself, but that wasn't much different than what she had done before.

Looking at her empty lunch table and to the other tables that were starting to fill up with students, she remembered how she used to feel embarrassed sitting alone. *But now it beats bleeding behind the school.*

She just needed to finish the school year out. Her father wasn't going to be able to pay for her tuition anymore. That was one small blessing out of it all.

From the moment she had walked through the school doors for the very first time, Elle had felt like she didn't fit into this prep school. She had been happy back in public school, and she wished her parents had never enrolled her there in the first place. The kids there only cared about the label stitched into their clothing, while all Elle worried about was if she was going to survive her first and final year here at Legacy Prep.

Doubtful.

The cafeteria slowly went suspiciously quiet as whispering began. Looking around the busy room, she saw everyone's attention on the door behind her.

Spinning around to see what had gained so much attention, Elle's eyes rested on a once beautiful girl who had the most gorgeous pair of striking gray eyes. Now, in her place, stood a girl with enflamed red slashes across her face and tortured gray eyes.

What happened to her?

"Fucking freak!" was said, followed by laughter filling the space with continuous echoes of the word "freak."

Elle's heart dropped as she watched the girl turn back around and leave the lunchroom. She didn't know who had yelled it, but she was sure Chloe had seen.

She stared down at her plate before squeezing the sides of her tray and quickly standing up, getting rid of its contents and heading out the door the marked girl had just left.

Seeing the swinging of the girls' bathroom door, she went inside what seemed an empty bathroom, but the feet under one of the stalls revealed otherwise.

Elle put her hand on the occupied stall to feel that it wasn't latched. "Chloe?"

Opening the door, she was able to see this new version of her up-close for the first time.

The once beautiful girl sat there, spilling silent, glowing red tears down her cheeks. She was right to think Chloe had once been beautiful, but now her beauty was truly breathtaking. You would think that the red slashes would have tainted her looks. However, it was the complete opposite. They let you see her true beauty: *her strength*.

Elle could see the torture Chloe had endured. She didn't think she could have survived it if she had suffered Chloe's fate.

Chloe looked up at Elle through blurry eyes, waiting for her to call her a freak just like the others. It wouldn't make her hurt any more than she already did.

I deserve it from her.

"Are you okay?"

What? She could see the true concern on her face and couldn't understand.

"W-why would you care after what I-I did to you?"

"We both know you wouldn't have done it if I didn't tell you to."

Chloe stared at Elle, even more confused.

"That doesn't make what I did any better."

"I think getting Mr. Fredrick's to find me does."

Elle stared at her, waiting to see if she would confirm that it was, in fact, her who had gotten her help. Though she didn't say anything, her silence answered the question.

"Do you think Sebastian, Cassandra, or the others would have gotten me help? How long do you think I would have been out there till someone found me?"

"I'm sorry I didn't do it sooner. I'm sorry for everything," Chloe whispered.

"I don't blame you. Sebastian and Cassandra are the only ones I blame."

Chloe stared up at her in disbelief. She wanted Elle to hate her or, at the very least, put some blame on her. She blamed herself.

Why doesn't she—

"They didn't do that to you, did they?"

Chloe quickly shook her head and started wringing her hands.

"What happened then?"

When Chloe didn't answer, Elle took a seat on the floor in front of her.

"W-What are you doing?"

Elle crossed her arms. "I'm going to sit here and wait till you're ready to tell me."

"But you're sitting on the bathroom floor."

"And you're sitting on a toilet." Giggling, she continued, "I would say that's both pretty gross."

A slight smile lifted Chloe's lips for the first time in what felt like ages. "That's true."

"Now, are you going to tell me, or are you going to make me sit here all day?"

Chloe took a deep breath, not looking up from her hands. "I w-was in a car wreck."

Staring at her intently, Elle studied her a moment before she replied, "No, you weren't. That's a lie."

"W-What! Y-Yes I wa—"

"Again, that's a lie," Elle responded. "You're a terrible liar, you know."

How would she know?

"Why do you think I'm l-lying?"

Elle shrugged. "Because I have to lie to my parents way more than I'd like to, and when you are a professional liar like me, it's easy to tell when someone is clearly lying straight to your face. Also … You are just really, really bad at lying."

Chloe looked down at her hands as Elle slightly chuckled at her lying skills. She didn't know what else to say other than what her father had embedded into her since she had woken up at the hospital.

"Okay, fine." Standing up off the floor, Elle started wiping off any dirt that might have stuck to the back of her jeans. "You were in a car wreck. For now, anyway … till you decide to spill."

Brrring.

The lunch bell sounded right on cue.

Elle reached her hand out to help Chloe up off the seat, and as her hand came close, Chloe let out a small scream.

Quickly, Elle pulled her hand back. "I'm sorry … I was just going to help you up."

Chloe covered her mouth and tried desperately to blink back the tears that started to fill her eyes, but she was unsuccessful.

I'm so screwed up. What's wrong with me? How am I supposed to go on with school or life now?

Sitting back down on the floor, it was like Elle could read her mind. "It's okay. We'll wait till you're ready to go back out there."

Silently crying, Chloe could only repeat the words that would forever be ingrained in her soul.

I was in a car wreck; that's all I know. I was in a car wreck. No one hurt me …

PAYBACK WAS A BITCH

The first day back to school was so horrible Chloe only hoped her second day wouldn't turn out as bad. Nevertheless, as she headed to her first period, it was going the exact same way.

Trying her best to block out the students, she headed straight to her class, and when she reached her classroom, she saw some of her old "friends" reading a newspaper.

Slowly heading to the back of the class, she began to feel nauseous as they started to laugh behind the newspaper, watching her sink into her seat.

"I told you she turned into a freak from a car wreck." Cassandra snickered, handing the newspaper off to some other students who had just come in.

"Bullshit. He swerved to miss a dog. Her father was probably drunk." Sebastian looked right at her. "Wasn't he?"

Not that night.

Chloe looked down at her lap to see she was digging her nails into her skin.

Sebastian stood and spoke more loudly. *"Wasn't he?"*

Hearing the snatching of a newspaper, she looked up to see Elle had taken the paper away from a nosey, little kid who was one step away from getting picked on himself if it weren't for Chloe being the main target in school.

Shoving the paper into her satchel, Elle took the seat right in front of Chloe, shielding her from their view.

"If her father was actually drunk, we would have all heard about it by now."

"Her father didn't even get a scratch, while she got her face all fucked up." Sebastian cackled.

Chloe tried to focus on the pain she was causing to her palm, but it wasn't working. She took each harsh word as a slap to the face.

"So he didn't get hurt. What's your point?" Elle glared at Sebastian .

Sebastian now stood, looking down at Elle. "So, my dad says he was drunk off his ass since drunk drivers are never the ones who get hurt because of the effect from the alcohol. He can't believe that her father won and hates everyone who voted for—"

"That's enough, kids! It's time to start class." The teacher walked in, finishing the conversation.

Brrring.

The loud bell had Chloe opening her hands to see little droplets of blood appear where her nails had dug into her skin.

She spent the class in her head, wishing that drunk driving were the cause of her "fucked up" face. Then she spent the next class trying to push away the memories of what had really happened. The battle continued until her third class started, and finally, when the lunch bell rang, Elle brought her out of her thoughts.

"Chloe, it's time for lunch. Are you okay?"

Looking around the now almost empty room, she stood, slowly nodding her head.

It took Elle a minute of staring her down before she decided to walk on to the cafeteria.

Walking beside the strawberry-blonde to lunch, she kept her head down. It was easier looking at the cold floor than the cold stares when everyone looked at her marked face. Despite not seeing them, she could still feel the stares as they tried to get a glimpse of her through her dark curtain of hair.

When they reached the lunch room, it was obvious it was pizza day, as the line was long and the other line of chicken patties and hamburgers was practically empty.

As Elle walked toward the chicken and hamburger line without a thought, Chloe stopped her.

"Wait, you don't want pizza?"

"Yes, but not enough to stand in line with them." She nodded her head toward the back of the line that held Cassandra and Sebastian, along with all the other kids who had helped beat her up.

"You're right." Chloe gulped at the thought.

Following Elle to the empty line, she couldn't help feeling like she would never be able to eat school pizza ever again. She could already sense her freedom of picking what to eat for lunch taken away from her.

After grabbing their lunches, she followed her once again to the table closest to the cafeteria door, the one she had watched Elle sit at alone every day. She sat in front of her so her back was to the filled lunchroom. This way, she wouldn't have to watch all the students staring at her and mocking her fresh cuts.

She remembered how bad she used to feel for Elle sitting all by herself. Never once had Chloe sat with her. *Because I was afraid.*

Wasn't it ironic?

She feared their judgment, but she had found out what true fear was. She used to feel bad for Elle, yet now she admired her uncaring attitude over whether they liked her or not. Payback was a bitch.

"You d-don't really get to pick what you w-want for lunch, do you?" Chloe asked, picking at her chicken patty and fries.

Popping a fry in her mouth, Elle seemed unbothered by her question. "Nope."

Bye, pizza.

"I guess you didn't get to pick what they said happened to you, either?" Elle continued.

"W-what does-s that mean?"

"They want you to say you were in a car wreck when you weren't. Who's making you say that?"

I wish.

"I-it did happen."

Giving her another long stare, Elle decided to say something this time. "What happened? Tell me what happened that night."

Looking down at her lap, Chloe started to wring her hands. A flash appeared in front of her as a blade started to inch closer and closer to her face. She quickly slammed her eyes shut.

"I-I don't remember."

"Okay. Then tell me to my face you don't remember."

Lifting her head up, she could feel her teary eyes betray her as lone tear slid down her cheek. Looking at Elle, she pictured her helpless, on the ground, bloody again.

I can't do it. She couldn't move her lips to lie to that girl again.

Understanding Chloe couldn't speak the words, Elle said, "I won't tell anyone, and when you're ready to tell me what happened, I'm here."

Minutes passed as Chloe continued to pick at her food before she began to wonder what had given her away when no one else in the world seemed to question what had happened that horrific night.

"How did you know?"

Elle stared into Chloe's now hollow gray depths. "Your eyes. I can tell someone not only marked you"—she pointed to her own face with a slicing motion—"but your soul."

Chloe closed her eyes as she tried desperately not to cry, picturing the demon who haunted her dreams.

Glancing at the table that held Sebastian and Cassandra, Elle continued, "I know that because I've been marked, too."

BURNED BY THE
HAND OF HR DEMON

Elle needed a book out of her locker, so Chloe went with her during break to retrieve it. The last class of the day seemed to come quickly after lunch. Surprisingly, they shared every class except the second one of the day. While she had art, Elle had health class. It sucked to not have the exact same schedule, but thankfully, it was only one class.

Watching Elle open the locker, she saw a rectangular piece of paper flutter to the ground.

"What the …?" Elle bent over to pick it up. Turning it over to the other side, her expression changed.

Chloe stared at what she thought was a piece of paper, but what was actually a photograph. The photo was of Elle lying on the pavement, bloody and broken, the exact image Chloe had thought of earlier. One of them must have snapped a photo of her when Chloe had been heading back into the school.

"W-who did this?"

They both looked around to see who had placed the photo, and they saw Sebastian standing against his locker, smiling evilly.

Elle quickly turned around, shoving the photo in her bag along with all her books. "Go get everything out of your locker."

"I h-had no idea he took t-that—"

"Go get your stuff," Elle ordered, continuing to clean out her locker.

"I d-didn't kno—"

The slamming of Elle's locker made her jump.

Taking a deep breath, Elle tried again, "I know you didn't. We need to get to class. He's not happy with me bashing him this morning about the whole car wreck thing, so he's letting me know he can beat the crap out of me again if he wanted."

Agreeing, Chloe quickly went to her locker, putting all the contents shakily into her bag.

"I'm sorry, E-Elle," she whispered.

"It's okay." Trying to make her feel better, she went to pat her shoulder.

A small gasp escaped Chloe's throat before she quickly moved out of the way.

Stepping back a bit, Elle held her hands up. "Sorry."

It took Chloe a moment before she went to put the last book from her locker into her bag and closed it.

"We need to get to class … fast."

Watching Elle swiftly leave with a sad look on her face, Chloe rubbed her shoulder where Elle's hand had almost touched her. It was like her skin burned. Burned by the hand of her demon.

Elle sat on her bed, staring down at the picture she had found in her locker today. It was strange to see herself that damaged on the pavement. She had looked at herself in the mirror after it had happened, but it was still strange to see it in person, as if she were looking down at herself in that moment when she had thought death was going to greet her.

A droplet of water fell from her cheek onto the photo. *Don't let them make you cry anymore.*

Getting up, she went to her bookshelf and grabbed a photo album off the shelf. Sitting back on her bed, she flipped through the pages, glancing at the photos of herself throughout the years.

She looked happy in every picture, and her long, strawberry-blonde hair used to frame her face perfectly.

Reaching up, she touched the strands she had left now that fell to the base of her neck.

Nope, don't you cry.

Finally going to the first blank page, she stuck the horrendous photo of herself that Sebastian had given her as a warning message into the photo album. She was going to remember this exact image of herself for the remainder of the school year. Then, when the new school year started at her new school, she could look back at this photo and thank God she had survived.

She closed the book. "I will survive."

Looking across the dinner table, Chloe watched her father pour more of the hard liquor into his glass.

He downed the contents the asked, "Are you going to s-s-stare at me o-or eat?"

"Eat, Chloe," her mother commanded.

Looking down at her plate, she picked up the fork to eat, but she had no appetite. The only reason she was sitting there and not in her room was because her mother had insisted.

"Quit acting like you're a victim," her mother's words rang through her head again.

She glanced back up when she heard the liquor bottle *ting* against his glass once more.

Quickly, she put her eyes back on the plate when he downed the contents in a split second.

Maxwell wiped his mouth with the back of his hand. "Go."

Stunned by his harsh voice, she couldn't move. He had sounded just like—

"Get the fuck out of my fac-c-ce!" He slammed his hand down on the table, making the silverware quiver. "I can't even-n-n look at you!"

Jumping up from the table, she tried not to trip as she started sprinting from the table like her life depended on it.

Her father became scarier by the day, each day reminding her more and more of the one who had given her nightmares.

Her eyes became cloudy, blurring her vision along the way. Once she reached her room, she slammed the door shut and leaned her back against the door before falling to the floor, sobbing.

She had asked herself many times, *Why me? Why did this happen to me?* But tonight, she had started asking herself a different question.

"Why couldn't I have died?"

THE MEMORY BANGING
AT THE DOOR

I t *was strange, but in* a short amount of time, she was becoming close with Elle. They understood each other as outcasts along with their suffering. The semester was almost up, and it was time for Christmas break. Chloe was going to really miss Elle, yet she wasn't going to miss school. However, she wasn't sure what was better at this point: her home life or school life.

Walking to their last class of the day, Chloe kept her head down. She walked closer to Elle than ever, letting Elle guide her through the hallways so she could keep her head down. Since the picture had showed up in Elle's locker, they didn't waste time in the hallways, and they were beginning to wonder if they were acting paranoid.

"Freak!" someone yelled out as she passed.

So the name-calling hadn't stopped, but at least they weren't too worried about their safety.

Reaching the science classroom, they took their seats in the back.

"Our science project is due before Christmas break. If we don't finish it today in class, then we will need to finish it up outside of school," Elle told her in a worried voice.

"Okay," she agreed, nervous about where this was going.

"Good. If we don't finish it, then we can finish it up at your house. Tomorrow sound okay?"

No...

"W-Why can't we do it at yours?"

Elle cleared her voice. "I'm sure you heard about my dad. My parents don't really want company right now ..."

Of course she knew what had happened to her dad. Cassandra had blabbed about it to the entire school at the beginning of the year.

"Come on, Chloe; it'll be fun. We should make it a sleepover!"

Instantly, she felt backed into a corner. The last word she would use to describe her house was fun. She knew Elle was taking the opportunity to help her come back out of her shell, to make her feel normal again. And while she wanted to desperately, her house wasn't the ideal place to do so. Nevertheless, it didn't sound like Elle's was, either. And since Elle was the one with a good excuse, she was screwed.

What am I supposed to say? My dad is now an alcoholic because he can't handle what happened to me any better than I can? Realizing her back had now hit the corner, her last hope was talking to her mother to keep her father controlled. If anything, the last thing they wanted was their appearance damaged.

"I-I'll ask my parents if you can come over, then."

"Awesome! Do you live in the little white house now?" Elle's eyes lit up.

She shook her head. "No, we won't move until January when my father gets sworn in."

Brrring.

The teacher stood from her desk. "All right, students, let's get to work. This is the last day you can work on your project in class, so make it count."

Chloe quickly went to work. She was going to work her ass off until the bell rang. That way, Elle wouldn't have to come over.

There is no way I am not going to finish this project.

Brrring.

She did not finish their project.

"Mom, Elle will be here any minute. Where are you?" she whispered into the phone.

"I'm running late at the office. I'll be home in an hour."

That was all Chloe heard before the *beep* came through the

phone, telling her that her mother had hung up.

Crap!

She was about to do that exact same thing in her pants as she watched her dad pick up his bottle to fill up his cup again. Her mother had advised her that she was a failure in the first place since she hadn't finished it at school. Then she had advised her to finish it up at Elle's, but when Chloe had explained Elle's situation, her mother had no longer cared.

Her mother had quickly realized Elle didn't come from money since she couldn't recall the last name of Buchanan having any real standing in Kansas City, Missouri. In turn, she couldn't give two shits what she thought about her family. However, her mother had promised her that she would keep Maxwell contained. Clearly, that was low on her to-do list.

Ding.

Just don't answer it. Maybe she will go away.

Ding.

"Are you ... going to ans-s-swer the damn ... door?" Maxwell started going toward the door himself.

Chloe quickly got up and passed him. "I can get—"

"I can get it myself!" He put his hand on Chloe as she passed him, pushing her forcefully out of the way.

Opening her mouth to scream as his hand made contact with her arm, only her breath came out as she fell to the floor.

All of a sudden, she could feel the rough hands holding her down while she tried to scream and fight them off her as she lay on the cold table.

The sound of the door opening and the cold air of the night touching her face brought her back to the present.

"Hello, Mr. Ma—Chloe, are you okay?" Elle's face had changed from a smile to concern as quickly as her tone did.

Staring at her face from the floor as Elle stood on the other side of the doorway, Chloe was too stunned to speak.

Maxwell took it upon himself to answer for her. "She's fine ... She tripped. Who are you ...?"

I tripped. No one hurt me.

Desperately trying to shake off the fall and the memory banging at the door in her head, she began to get up to avoid raising any alarms for Elle.

"Um, I'm Elle. We are supposed to finish our science project." Her eyes danced between father and daughter.

"Do-Don't you r-remember?"

"No, because-s-she you didn't tell ... me." He went back to fetch his alcohol. "Get rid of her," he voiced to Chloe as he walked past, uncaring if the girl at the door heard.

Putting her eyes on the floor, Chloe did as she was asked. "I-I'm sorry. Now's not a g-good time."

Elle waited until Maxwell was no longer seen and hopefully out of earshot before she went up to Chloe, whispering, "Are you okay? What happened?"

"Yes, I-I tripped."

"Bullcrap!" Elle whispered harshly. "I'm calling my mom to

come back. You can come home with me."

"No, I'm fine!"

Elle pulled out her cell phone, not listening to Chloe's pleas, and told her mom to come back. Once she hung up the phone, she addressed Chloe again.

"Is he the one who hurt you?"

Shaking her head, she looked back at the floor.

"And I'm supposed to believe you!"

"Yes. He's just been drinking. T-that's how he handles what … happened to me."

Knowing she was telling the truth, Elle relaxed just a smudge. "You're still coming with me."

"N-no, really. It's okay. I swear he's never physically hurt me before. My falling was an accident." *I'm sure he didn't mean to.* "Mom is almost home. I don't want to leave him alone."

She could see the wheels turning in Elle's head before she nodded. "Okay, I'll ask my mom if you can come over to my house tomorrow to finish our project."

"I thought you said your parents didn't want company over?"

"Yeah, well, I lied," Elle answered as she headed back out the door. "See you tomorrow."

"Um, okay …" Chloe closed the door behind her when she saw Elle's mom pulling back into the driveway.

Heading back into the house, she hoped that she could tiptoe up to her room unnoticed.

"Sit down, Chloe."

Stopping in her tracks, she saw her father sitting at the dining room table. She also noticed his tone had changed to a somewhat more pleasant one. *Maybe he wants to apologize...*

Taking the seat in front of him, she sat down at the table.

"Does she know what really happened to you ...?" He took a sip from his glass.

Chloe violently shook her head, scared of where this was heading.

"Why not? It's written all ... over the paper what really hap-p-p-pened to you."

Staring at him, she didn't know what to say.

He quickly reminded her, "Tell me what happened to you, Chloe."

Wringing her hands, she began to dig her nails into her palms. "I was in a car wreck; that's all I know. I was in a car wreck. No one hurt me."

IF I CAN'T TELL YOU I'M SCARED OF YOU, OR IF . . . YOU JUST BECAME MY NEW BFF

Letting Chloe spend the night at Elle's the next day was her parents' way of making it up to her after what had happened. Plus, the girls really did have to finish their project if they didn't want a big fat F.

Her mother driving her to Elle's house consisted of straight complaints since it wasn't in "the suburbs" and was too far out for her "taste." Chloe had just kept her mouth shut and was thankful when they reached their destination.

Walking up to the house, Chloe felt embarrassed to see Elle again after what had happened. She just hoped they could pretend yesterday hadn't happened. *That's what I'm going to do, at least.*

Before getting to the door, she could see Elle peeking her head out the front window of the house, and then she was gone.

"Hi!" Elle opened the door wide for her.

Cracking a small smile was the best she could do with her nerves. She was still not used to showing her face, and she wasn't sure how Elle's parents would react to her scars.

As soon as she came through the door, she was pretty much in the living room, and the first thing she noticed was a cute, little boy playing on the floor with his cars. Her eyes then went to the wheelchair that held a man who was watching his son play beside him. Chloe had known what to expect, but seeing it was different.

Finally, when he looked up, she expected his face to turn to shock, if even for a moment, but it didn't.

"This is my dad and my little brother Josh, and this is Chloe Masters," Elle made the introductions quickly, pointing to the person the name correlated to.

Josh didn't look up from his toys.

Chloe only nodded her head, not wanting to stutter out a hello first to her dad. Another shocking thing happened when he just nodded his head and went back to watching his son play.

She saw it right before his eyes left hers—an understanding. The understanding was one of loss, and she could feel he wasn't any used to his new body than she was.

From what Chloe knew—*thanks to big mouth*—was that he had suffered a forklift accident and lost the use of his legs, which had happened during the beginning of the school year. He had gained a huge promotion at the factory before the accident and had pulled Elle from public to private school. So, Elle being new at school this year had made the perfect target for Cassandra. Hence, why they were all here at this moment.

"Hello!" A sweet and very pretty woman wearing an apron came from the kitchen.

Elle smiled. "And this is my mom, of course."

"I would give you a hug, but Elle already warned me you're not a hugger like me."

Chloe looked over at Elle, even more nervous now.

"Yeah, I told them you were a germaphobe. You know, touching creeps you out because of germs." Elle gave her a look, wanting her to play along.

Genius.

She began nodding her head. "Y-Yep. Sorry about t-that."

"That's okay, sweetie; no need to be sorry. I'm just glad one of Elle's friends was finally able to come over. I keep telling her she can have a big sleepover with all her little girlfriends at school."

Excuse me?

"Oh, Mom, you know I will one day."

Say what?

"Are you on the soccer team with Elle?"

No thought came to her. Blinking and trying to figure out if this conversation was real was the only thing she could do.

Her mother laughed. "Sorry. I forgot—germaphobe."

"Yeah, Mom, she doesn't like getting dirty. Okay, well, we've got a bunch of work to do." Elle headed toward a hall. "Come on, Chloe."

Realizing this was very real, she quickly went after Elle, not saying another word. Frankly, she had no clue how on earth to respond.

Once they were in her bedroom, Elle went straight to her backpack on her bed, pulling out their project materials.

"Um, Elle ...?"

"Yeah?"

"You really are a good liar."

The strawberry-blonde flashed a smile. "It's a gift."

Chloe blinked a few more times, looking at this side of her she hadn't known existed. "I can't tell if I'm scared of you or if ... You just became my new BFF."

Elle laughed. "BFF, for sure. Of course, you want to be best friends with the most popular girl in school. Uh ... duh!"

"Just as long as you tell all of your friends that I'm your best friend." She began laughing with her.

Their relationship had just changed for the better. Within a matter of minutes, she felt extremely comfortable around Elle. It just felt right.

"Deal!"

They laughed so hard they started to cry.

"How come you haven't invited your best friend to any of your soccer games?"

Elle wiped away a tear. "I hear the stands are really germy."

"Where on earth did you get germaphobe from?"

"Web MD."

The two laughed until their faces and stomachs began to hurt, and then finally, they were able to stop their laughing fit.

Elle wiped away the final tear. "It also says we might have cancer."

STUCK BETWEEN REALITIES

Chloe lay stiffly in the bed, staring at the white ceiling. She hadn't thought this far into a sleepover.

Her sleep had been non-existent, but when she did, the nightmares came for her. She had gone many nights without sleep since what had happened to her, and she was going to do that tonight.

Staring at the blank ceiling for hours, she watched her nightmare play before her, unmoving like she had done every night, praying sleep would never come to throw her to the devil once again.

The screams were what first brought Elle out of her deep sleep. The violent shaking of the bed was what had completely awakened her.

Sitting up in bed, Elle looked down at the sleeping girl beside her. In sleep was where you found peace, but the dark-haired girl looked like she had found the opposite: torture. Even in the night, she could see the glistening tears that fell from Chloe's hollow eyes and pained face.

"Chloe ... Chloe ..." She hoped her voice would be enough to wake her, not wanting to touch her, afraid it would make the nightmare worse.

Chills ran up her spine from witnessing what seemed like possession.

"Chloe!" She reached out...

The cold, metal table underneath her was a stark contrast to her burning face from what seemed like pointless crying.

"Please! Stop!" No amount of her kicking and fighting was a match for what felt like millions of hands holding her down.

The laughter from the evil man who held a knife rang through her ears, mocking.

"Stay still, little girl"—he drew the knife closer to her face—"or it'll just hurt worse."

Looking at his abnormally large, black eyes, she was sure she was looking into the eyes of the devil ...

"Chloe!"

Waking up to a hand coming for her, she jumped up from the bed. Her breathing was heavy and rushed, feeling as if she were slowly suffocating. She couldn't catch her breath.

Elle quickly turned on the bedside lamp so she could see she was no longer in her nightmare. Then she ran toward Chloe's side.

"It's okay. It was just a dream. Breathe, Chloe."

Taking deep breaths and looking around at her surroundings, Chloe realized she was no longer trapped in her nightmare.

Exhausted, she sank to the floor, holding her knees to her chest and silently crying into them, unable to show her face to Elle. She knew what Elle would think of her now. *Freak.*

Her skin still crawled from the devil's touch. That was how vivid her nightmares were. It was as if she were reliving it all again.

Elle sat on the floor beside her, making sure there was plenty of space between them. "What you dreamed about really happened to you, didn't it?"

Chloe didn't respond, continuing her silent cries.

Taking that as a yes, Elle asked a different question, "Will you tell me what happened?"

Again, no response.

Elle took a deep breath. "I come home every day and lie straight to my parents' faces, telling them about all my friends and how I had such a great day at school. It's a heck of a lot easier than telling them how scared I am at school to even use the girls' bathroom.

"When the kids started getting violent, that's when I told them I joined the soccer team. It helped explain why I was getting bruises every time I was pushed into a locker or whatever mean thing they had planned for me that day.

"My parents believe whatever lie I tell them because they haven't figured out how to handle my father becoming paralyzed yet. My dad's addicted to his painkillers, so it's like he's not even here, and my mom is working as much as she can to support us all, along with caring for Josh and now Dad. I help with whatever I can when I get home, but I mostly fade into the background. I can care for myself, and I pretend that everything is fine."

Chloe looked up to see that some tears had fallen down Elle's face.

"I have a feeling that whatever happened to you doesn't compare to what happened to me behind the school that day. But I do understand what you're going through more than anyone else probably.

"When I came over to your house yesterday, I thought your dad's drinking might be like my dad with painkillers, but now I'm not so sure. I asked my dad to take it easy since you were coming over, and he did. His pills also don't make him mean; they just make him non-existent."

Chloe didn't know what to say.

"Now that you know all my secrets, whatever you tell me about what happened to you or about what it's like at home, I swear that I will *never, ever* tell *anyone*. I lie and pretend every day, too, and I don't want my parents to suffer with the truth, and I definitely don't want Cassandra or Sebastian to find out that my dad is addicted to pills. I wished every night to find someone to talk to so I know that it's real, and now I can with you."

So I know that it's real . . . That was Chloe's problem; she was stuck between realities, questioning if her nightmares or what they said in the papers was real.

It was as if Elle could read her thoughts.

"What everyone is saying happened to you isn't real. The car wreck wasn't real. No one knows what really happened to you, but now you can tell someone you can trust."

Chloe knew, if she were going to ever tell anyone, it would be Elle. She believed her when she had said she would never tell, and they did relate to each other in many ways. She'd had no clue of the extent of Elle's suffering, and she was glad she had told her everything.

Chloe wanted to tell her, but she was afraid to, because once she said it out loud, she couldn't take it back. Once the words were spoken... *Then it is real.*

"What really happened to you, Chloe?"

Taking a deep breath, she mustered up enough courage to unzip the thin jacket she had worn to bed. Slowly, she removed the jacket and revealed the various scars that marked her arms. This was the first time she had revealed the fact that she wasn't just marked on her face.

Elle covered her mouth in shock, having no clue Chloe had been hiding further injuries.

Wiping away the tears on her face, Chloe rested the back of her head on the wall. Then she looked up at the white ceiling, her nightmare starting to play from the beginning.

"T-The day you got beaten up was the n-night ... I got my scars."

THE MURDER OF ELLE BUCHANAN

he crazy events of the weekend had come and gone, just like their last week of school. Sitting in science class, the final class of the semester, they turned in the project they had finished at Elle's.

Chloe had an emotional breakdown that night after she had awoken from her nightmare and become vulnerable enough to reveal her dark secrets. She had ended up telling Elle everything that had happened to her that horrible night. She had also told her about her parents and what it was like for her at home. Thankfully, Chloe didn't regret it. She and Elle were in the same boat of secrets and had nowhere to turn except each other.

She's the only one I will ever tell.

Chloe looked up to Elle. She was strong, whereas Chloe was not. She didn't show her fear to the world, whereas she did. Therefore, she found herself depending on Elle to survive this hell and to keep her sanity. At this point in her life, at its lowest, the most important thing to her was their friendship.

Brrring.

Quickly, all the students ran out of the classroom, eager for Christmas break. Even the teachers were scurrying to leave.

Elle and Chloe continued to stay put, waiting for the hallways to clear. They were being extra careful because, now being two, their target was bigger.

"You're going to come and spend the night at my house during the break, right?" Elle asked.

Um ...

Laughing, Elle could see what she was thinking. "Next time, we can stay up all night, watching movies. We will just pull all-nighters, so no need to sleep."

Chloe's lips turned up into a smile. "Okay, deal."

"I think it should be good now."

They both stood, gathering their things, and ventured out into the hall. Chloe followed a step behind her, and even though the hallways were pretty much cleared out, she still kept her head toward the ground. The science class was in the back of the school, so they had a good distance to go, and Chloe didn't want to take the chance of someone mocking her face on the way out for the last time.

They were getting closer to the front of the school and only had one turn left to get out of the halls. When Elle took the sharp turn first, Chloe heard the massive *whack* that sent Elle flying back to her butt.

As she held her nose, the blood started to trickle down her hand and face.

Chloe felt every muscle in her body freeze as she looked at the twisted expression on Sebastian's face with a big biology book in his hands. Her mouth dropped open to scream, but a cold hand appeared over her lips, keeping her silenced.

The devil's voice whispered in her ear, *"Stay still, little girl."*

Chills ran up her spine as she waited for her turn from Sebastian's wrath. She knew she should move, run, or help. She could feel something deep down inside of her screaming at her to do just that. However, it was as if the devil's hands were holding her still. She could feel them gripping her wrists.

"You need to fucking keep your eyes to yourself, bitch."

Elle's shirt was getting stained redder and redder by the second.

"I wasn't going to say anything. I don't care what you do."

"What the fuck did you just say to me? You don't care what I do?" Sebastian went to smash the book over Elle, but she covered her head just in time.

The book smashed into her forearm hard enough to hear a small crack.

"Keep your fucking mouth shut, both of you." He looked at Chloe and raised the book again.

The invisible hands cuffed her wrists more securely, causing tears to brim her eyes.

"Or it'll just hurt worse."

Elle grabbed Sebastian's leg. "No …!"

"Don't you tell me no." Sebastian reared the book back toward Elle again, giving her barely enough time to cover her head. He connected the book to the same arm, but this time, the cracking sound was much louder, solidifying a break in the arm.

A smug look crossed his face as he left.

"You're one lucky, little girl," he whispered before his invisible hands slowly disappeared.

"Chloe …? Chloe, are you all right?" Elle's pained voice finally rang through her ears.

Blinking away the tears in her eyes that rained down her cheeks, making her scars glisten red, she looked down at Elle. She was able to see the destruction Sebastian had caused once again.

"I-I'm s-so sorry. I t-tried to—" She began to violently shake.

"I know you did." Elle slowly got up off the floor, careful not to put any pressure on her hurt limb. "I'll be okay."

She wiped the tears off her face when Elle did the same and then looked around, expecting someone to come help.

Elle used the arm of her black hoodie to wipe some of the blood off her face. "No one's coming." Then she zipped up the rest of her hoodie to cover her blood-splattered shirt and put up the hood using her good arm. "No one cares."

Looking around once more, it looked as if the hallways had been deserted years ago.

She's right; I couldn't even care enough to help her.

The tears blurred her vision again, but she tried her best to push them back down. "Why did he do it?"

Holding her broken arm to her chest, Elle winced. "When we came out of class, I saw him buying weed off a senior in the halls. I thought I turned my head away fast enough, but I guess not."

That was why she had no clue what had pissed him off and why he had wanted them to keep their mouths shut. She always kept her head to the ground, so she never noticed what went on in the halls and didn't see the faces of those who called her a freak.

Chloe picked up Elle's satchel from the ground and put it on her shoulder with her own book bag. "Come on. I'll walk to the hospital with you."

The hospital was thankfully just a street over from the school.

"But isn't your mom waiting to pick you up outside?" Elle asked.

"No, she's always an hour late. I'll text her to pick me up there."

Elle nodded. "I'll call my mom and tell her when we get there that my last indoor soccer game didn't go so well."

It was wrong for them to chuckle at that, but the two had to make light of the situation somehow.

Walking through the rest of the school, Chloe noticed how the teachers turned their heads or ducked into a room as they passed. There was one fact Cassandra and Sebastian Ross made clear to the whole school the moment they had first walked through the school doors, and that was how their father had funneled donation money to the school. The principal and the teachers would look away from the murder of Elle Buchanan for a million dollars. The beating of a girl whose parents couldn't afford to donate a dime came at a much cheaper price.

No one ever fucked with the Ross's, and no one ever would, because the Ross's were one of the richest families in Kansas City, if not the richest.

"Why'd you do it?" Chloe quietly asked her.

"Do what?"

"Stop him from hitting me."

Elle waited until they reached the freedom from the school before she spoke.

"I haven't been able to sleep since you told me, and I'm hoping now I'll be able to get one night's rest without having my own nightmares of what happened to you."

SO HELP ME GOD

Staring at her new bedroom, in her new house, it should have brought her peace to start over fresh with the New Year ringing in. It didn't. It just solidified what she had lost, and now she added the house she had grown up in to that list.

A knock on the door came a moment before the door swung open.

"Ready?" her dad asked.

Wringing her hands, she tried to give it one more shot. "You can't tell them that I'm sick?"

The door came to a close as her father stepped into the room. "No. Get fucking used to the spotlight. Now come on."

Feeling the impending doom in her stomach, she stood and adjusted her black dress that her mother had picked out with long sleeves to cover up the real horror show she was.

"Remember, none of that germaphobe bullshit. Suck it up and

pretend to like it when they shake your hand. Do you understand me?"

Solemnly, she nodded.

"And try not to stutter," he added harshly.

"Yes, Father."

When Maxwell was satisfied, he opened the door for them to leave.

Walking through the house, she felt the bile in her stomach started to rise. The city liked to call it "the little white house," but to her, it seemed like the opposite. Everything was so white, cold, and empty that it made her feel as if she were locked up in an insane asylum.

I am … and the people who were holding her hostage there certainly made her feel as if she would be classified as insane.

Hearing the commotion draw closer, she wanted to turn back. However, her father was a step behind her, watching her every move. She had no option except to face what was coming.

Reaching the room, she saw there were TV crews and cameras filling up the space. Again, if it weren't for her father behind her, she couldn't have made it to her place beside her mother.

The ceremony started within minutes. A man handed a Bible over to her mother, and she watched as her father placed his hand upon it.

"I do solemnly swear that I will support the Constitution of the United States, the Constitution and Laws of the State of Missouri, and the Laws and Ordinances of the City of Kansas City, Missouri, and that I will, to the best of my ability, faithfully perform the duties of the Office of Mayor in the City of Kansas City, Missouri, during my continuance therein." Maxwell paused for just a moment. "So help me God."

At that moment, Chloe tried her best to smile next to her parents as the cameras began flashing a mile a minute. The oath her father had just taken solidified the truth of what had happened to her never coming to the light. Maxwell had successfully achieved everything he had been working for to become the mayor of Kansas City, and it had come with a price.

The devil had come to make him pay in his daughter's blood.

A small part of her hadn't thought he could take the oath after what had happened that night, but she had been wrong. Maxwell had just swept it under the rug, and all of Kansas City would never know the devil himself resided there.

"Congratulations, Mr. Mayor."

Another pit in her stomach began as the congratulatory handshakes started.

"Happy New Year, Mrs. Masters."

She took a small step back. *Please ignore me.*

A hand extended out to her. "Happy New Year to you, too, Chloe."

Staring at the manly hand extended to her, her mouth ran dry. She could feel her father's harsh gaze on her.

She slightly lifted her hand before putting it back down. "I-I'm sorry. I'm a g-germaphobe." She made sure to say it just loudly enough for people to hear so that it would spread by gossip, or if she were lucky, the newspaper. That way, she would never have to shake a hand ever again, and that was a win she needed, being the mayor's daughter. The amount of places and events she was going to be forced to attend to shake the hands of strangers in the future was something she didn't want to think about.

The room had gone silent at her words, and the focus had been drawn to her, scaring her shitless. The people around the room all looked as if they were examining the scars on her face and thinking one unison thought: *freak*.

She felt it then, the bile slowly creeping up her throat.

"Excuse m-me."

Running out the room, she could hear her father explaining how she had been feeling under the weather. She could hear his unspoken words that were just for her, telling her that she should be afraid. Very, very afraid.

Managing to keep from vomiting, she went to her room as quickly as she could and locked the door behind her. Her breathing was heavy as she backed away from the door, wondering if she had made the right choice.

There was only one way to find out.

He took a swig of his beer and sat back in his chair, smiling at the TV screen. The sight of her brought back the feelings he'd had the last time he had seen her. He thought his work looked beautiful on her, and he felt satisfied that, every time she looked in the mirror ... *She sees me.*

Laughing wickedly, he could tell, even though he was no longer physically hurting her, she was fucked up mentally.

"I told you it would just hurt worse, little girl."

The loud banging on the door had her hiding under the covers.

"Unlock this goddamn door right now!"

Even though Maxwell had learned how to become a functioning alcoholic over the past few weeks, she could hear the drinks he had consumed tonight in his bellowing voice.

"You embarrassed the hell out of me and your mother tonight!"

Fear started to creep in as it went quiet. She had greatly underestimated her father's wrath, and she just prayed she was going to survive.

Boom.

A body slammed into the door.

Chloe had been wrong.

Tears streamed down her face, caught upon her pillow that was now getting soaked.

"If you don't open this fucking door right now, so help me God, I'll make it worse for you."

The whisper of hands cuffed her wrists. *"Stay still, little girl, or it'll just hurt worse."*

Her father was becoming the devil's disciple. The fear she felt inside of her rivaled the fear she had felt while standing in the presence of the devil.

Bam.

The door flung open, and pure rage filled the room

Chloe held on tightly to the covers as she furiously held her eyes shut, hoping this was all just another nightmare.

Maxwell stalked to her bed. "Let this be your first lesson."

A second later, Chloe felt him roughly pick her up with her blanket before he threw her across the room a second later. Being touched through the covers didn't burn her skin like it would have if he had touched her flesh, but it still hurt.

The blanket had broken most of her fall, but she did take a good bang to the head against the wall.

Sitting up, she watched her father through tears as he walked over to her. The sight of him made her blood run cold.

"You're going to learn that crying won't help you. I'm done listening to it."

One final tear rolled down her cheek. Chloe didn't know it, but it would be the last tear she would shed.

Maxwell moved while she closed her eyes.

So help me God.

WATCHING YOUR BEST FRIEND
TURN INTO A MONSTER

Walking *up to the school* after Christmas break gave Chloe mixed feelings. Her father had mentally tortured her every night, and the night of his swearing in, he had stepped it up a notch. She hadn't cried a tear since realizing her father was right: Crying didn't erase her past. Crying didn't make touch easier for her to take. Crying didn't make the nightmares stop. Crying had never once saved her or made one thing easier for her.

It was as if she had used all of her tears up. Her eyes had run dry, and there was nothing left to cry for.

Yes, she was able to get away from the insane asylum, but this wasn't any better.

"Still a freak, I see." Cassandra giggled to her little group as they passed for obvious reasons.

But there was one silver lining. The best part about her life was here, and that was Elle. She had missed her a lot and hadn't had a chance to visit Elle over the break due to moving and her father's new position. She hoped, now that school had started back again, the excuse of projects and homework would help her.

Surprisingly, she found Elle waiting at the front of the school on one of the benches.

"Why is your face bruised?"

How could she tell that fast? Chloe had thought she had expertly put on some concealer and foundation to hide it.

"I didn't think it was that obvious," she whispered to her.

"It's not, but I can tell because I've had to do the same thing," Elle admitted. "Now, what happened?"

"I-I uh ... tripped again."

Elle went silent understanding what Chloe had meant before she quickly got up and started heading into the school. The last time they had walked the halls, it had turned bloody, so Chloe now started walking directly behind Elle, using her as a shield. It was easier for her this way, looking down at Elle's feet, following right behind. *At least no one will see the school freak coming right at them.*

They didn't talk about her bruises once as the day went on, and even though Chloe should have lied to Elle, there wasn't much of a point. She always knew when she was lying.

With her going to Art next and Elle going to Health, she expected them to go their separate ways, but Elle continued to lead the way to Art class. *What is she doing?*

"Wait here when class is over. I'll get over here as quickly as I can," Elle told her as she reached the Art room.

"It's too far; you shouldn't."

"I'll be fine, just wait."

"No, I can—"

"What are you going to do when Sebastian takes a book to your face or drags you outside so everyone can beat up on you? Are you going to be able to take it?"

Looking down at her hands, she started wringing them. She knew the answer; they both did. She didn't want to say it, though.

"I'll meet you here," Elle told her before she whisked away.

Walking into her classroom, Chloe felt defeated. She wanted to be strong like Elle, but anything strong in her had died the day she had been taken.

Taking a seat at her table that once remained empty before her scars, she looked at the table that held Cassandra and her other old friends. The empty seat beside Cassandra had once been hers. Chloe had gone from sitting at the cool kids table to the table no one would ever dare to sit at because that was where the school freak sat.

It was strange to show up at school and lose every friend you'd ever had because of the way you looked. It was even stranger to lose the one friend you'd had since kindergarten . . .

"That's mine!" Chloe told the little boy who had just snatched away the beautiful picture book she was flipping through.

When the boy had run away with it, laughing, she wanted to run and tell the teacher, but with it being her first day of school, she was afraid they would start to call her tattle tale and begin to make fun of her.

She began to pout in the corner by herself, but a blonde girl came over and handed the picture book back to her.

"I'm sorry. Sometimes, my bubby can be mean."

Chloe gave her a hug. "Thank you! Do you want to play with me?"

"Yes." The little girl smiled at her. "My name's Cassandra. What's yours?"

"Chloe."

Then another memory bombarded her.

"Can you believe we will be in high school next year!" Cassandra had practically squealed it in her ear with excitement.

The two had dreamed about high school for years and had endless conversations about the day they could finally attend Legacy Prep High.

"I know! I can't wait." She smiled, hoping it was going to be everything they dreamed of . . .

The memories made her realize it wasn't strange, but it was sad. Their relationship had gone downhill when her father had started running for mayor as a democratic candidate. Cassandra's father, being a strong republican, had said many harsh things about her father, and eventually, she believed it had started rubbing off on Cassandra. Then, when their dreams had come true of becoming a freshman, she could see that Cassandra had changed during summer break. Cassandra was determined to make her high school fantasies come to life, no matter the cost, and she wanted to take Chloe with her.

Chloe didn't want to become the most popular girl in school the way she did. Cassandra had wanted to do it dirty by bullying girls like Elle and now her. It had been hard for Chloe. She hadn't wanted to lose her friendship at first. And then, when Cassandra had become unpredictable, Chloe had been scared to get in her way or, worse, be on the receiving end. So now she agreed that it was sad watching your best friend turn into a monster.

Now, sitting at the freak table and looking at the cool kids table, she didn't miss it. *Not for a second.* She had known in her heart she didn't belong with them when they had boarded the bully train. They had drifted apart for too long, and it was only a matter of time before she was their next victim. The scars had just given her the ticket.

Brrring.

The Art closet door was flung open, and a tall, blond freshman who was way too good-looking for his own good exited the closet with a smirk on his face. A sophomore girl came out behind him, slightly embarrassed but not embarrassed enough to wipe her mouth to show the two had been making out. *Well, I hope just making out.*

Vincent Vitale was every girl's dream, and he knew it, too. His looks along with his confidence got him any girl he wanted in school, even the seniors.

He took his seat next to one of his best friends who wasn't nearly as tall or as fortunate looking as him, Amo.

Amo was just exactly as you would think a freshman boy would look: awkward.

Looking back at her once best friend, she wished girls got along like boys did. They were simple and couldn't care less what their male friends looked like. She was pretty sure, if one of them showed up with her scars, the other boy would have thought it was gruesome but fascinating at the same time.

Watching the sophomore girl take her old seat next to Cassandra, she saw the little sneer on her face, showing Chloe that she was rising in the ranks.

Chloe thought about the girl who would rather get a broken arm than see her hurt. She didn't miss it. *Not for a second.*

Elle sat down in the safety of her seat, out of breath from practically running to her class. She could see it written all over Chloe's face what she thought of her. Hell, Elle wanted her to think that; it was the only way Chloe was going to survive the rest of the year.

She thinks I'm strong, but I'm not.

It was all a façade, because deep down, she was one scared little girl. However, Elle had a time limit in this place, whereas Chloe's was endless. Chloe had barely mentioned the possibility of transferring schools or even becoming home-schooled, and her parents had dismissed her to her room for the whole day without lunch or dinner.

The sand in Elle's hourglass had now drained halfway down, and it was as if Chloe's hourglass was broken on a constant loop, the sand pouring down, only for it not to fill the bottom. That was why Elle was been protecting her—because just like her hourglass, she was broken. There was no way Chloe would be able survive without her. *She will break for good with no hope of return.* But Elle could at least postpone the inevitable or, by some miracle, help put her back together enough to survive this place.

I just hope I have enough time to fix her and not enough time to break me.

TICK TOCK

Tick. Tock.

Don't look at the clock.

One hourglass stands with barely any time left, draining so quickly the nightmare is almost over.

Tick. Tock.

Don't look at the other clock.

This hourglass stands still, broken, and suffering from the same loop, the nightmare only growing worse.

Tick. Tock.

Don't look at the clocks.

ALL WOUNDS HEAL WITH TIME

While Elle sat on her bed, her eyes grew tired from the countless studying. She had a big test in Science class tomorrow, and she really needed to get an A.

A little knock came to the door before her mother opened it. "Elle, sweetie, it's late."

"I have a big test tomorrow."

Her mother came into the room and took a seat on the bed in front of her. "I've noticed you've been obsessed with your grades lately. You know we are proud of you no matter what, and I don't want you to stress so much."

"I know." Elle smiled. "I'm just trying to make sure I give it my best so I can keep my options open in the future."

"With what?"

"You know … for college and stuff."

"Okay, sweetie." Her mother smiled back before she reached into her robe pocket and pulled out a picture. "I developed some pictures today and thought you might want to put them in your photo album."

Staring down at the photo, Elle's eyes were immediately drawn to Chloe. Even though her scar had healed a bit since then, you could still see the same amount of torture in her eyes today.

"This was when she first came over for our science project."

"Yep." Her mom patted her leg before she got up. "Now get some rest. You want to at least be awake during the test to get an A."

"Mom," Elle stopped her before she could close the door. "Thank you."

"You're welcome, sweetie."

Getting up out of bed, she went to her bookshelf and pulled out her photo album then set it on her bed. Elle flipped through the pages before she came to an abrupt stop at the picture Sebastian had given her as a warning message. Despite her wanting to sear this image of her bloody and bruised body into her brain, every day with Chloe, it started to fade.

Slowly, she started to place the picture of her and Chloe over it, covering the heinous picture and replacing it with something good.

Gone, but not forgotten.

Looking down at the new picture, she finally looked at herself. Her hair had grown quite a bit in a short amount of time, and it now grazed the top of her shoulders, showing her that all wounds heal with time, even though time wasn't on their side ...

"We will survive"—Elle closed the book with one last glance at the photo—"together."

THE LAST GRAIN OF
SAND HAD FALLEN

*T*ick. *Tock.*

Don't look at the clock.

An hourglass was still broken.

Tick. Tock.

Look at the other clock.

The last grain of sand had fallen.

Tick—

Time was up.

THE END OR JUST THE BEGINNING

t was either going to be the end or just the beginning for Elle. She had made her choice, and now the last piece of the puzzle needed to be added.

Looking at the newspaper on the bus, she saw all the X marks she had made under the classifieds. There was only one place left on the list, and if they turned her away, she wasn't sure what she was going to do.

The bus stopping had her getting up to exit, and once she was off the bus, she started second-guessing the whole thing. Downtown Kansas City didn't seem like a place for a newly fifteen-year-old girl who was alone. Thankfully, it was a quick walk to her destination.

Elle stopped to stare at the diner, looking up at the sign. The D flashed off and on, spelling out "Diner" or "Iner," depending on the moment you looked at it. She was able to clearly look inside since it seemed like nothing but windows revealing it was very outdated and needed a major deep clean. Finally, her eyes rested on the "Help Wanted" sign that was placed on the door.

In that moment, staring at the sign, a feeling of determination came over her. No matter what, she was going to get what she wanted. She didn't care how many lies came out of her mouth; it was hers.

Walking up to the door, she pushed on it, taking the first step inside.

That was the moment she decided to flip both hourglasses, causing both to start over. *The beginning.*

THAT WAS PRE-PUBESCENT AMO. PUBERTY AMO WILL BE A JERK

Chloe was, of course, the first one to take her seat or even reach the first class of the day. Beginning to wring her hands, she wondered why she had even tried to look nice today. Her makeup couldn't cover up the fact that she was a freak, and her long-sleeved, black shirt that matched her black jeans to perfection made her look crazy, considering it was warm outside.

Black was the only color that suited her anymore. It helped her fade into the background, just the way she wanted, and she still hadn't revealed to the world her other markings. For some dumb reason, she hoped that, since it was a new year, she could finally blend into the background.

The rest of her school days were going to be hell without Elle.

She didn't know how or even if she could do it, but there wasn't an option. *Sophomore year won't be the same without her...* Chloe had nothing and no one to save her. She was trapped and set to die in this school. Elle was at least free, and that made a part of her happy for once. *One of us made it out alive.*

"You look really pretty today," A sweet voice standing over her told her.

Chloe hated to look up and see who was about to make fun of her. The last thing she ever got was a compliment, so she knew it was going to turn into a cruel joke. She almost didn't look, but when she did, her mouth dropped open.

"W-Why are you here? You're not supposed to be here."

Elle crossed her arms with a smirk on her face. "You don't want me here?"

Utter confusion came over Chloe. "I don't understand."

"Well, I got a scholarship for my grades to pay part of my tuition, and I got a job to pay the rest of it." She took a seat in front of her. "You don't seem very happy. You're supposed to be happy."

"I'm n-not. You don't deserve to be here ... because of me." If Chloe could still cry, she was sure this was a moment in her life when she would. She had hated herself all last year when Elle had been her punching bag, and now she was back here again. Chloe was still too weak and broken to take up for herself and knew it was all going to happen again, no matter how much she hated herself for it.

"That's why I didn't tell you I was coming back. I was afraid you might talk me out of it somehow."

"I am. You're transferring back."

Elle laughed. "Won't work now. It would look really strange to my parents, and I would just have to tell them the truth about what happened to you and why I felt it necessary to come back here for you."

No, no, no, no! She began shaking her head.

"It's too late, Chloe."

She continued shaking her head back and forth. "Why are you doing this?"

Elle turned around in her desk, facing the front. "Because you need me." Looking back over her shoulder for just a moment, she revealed another truth, "And I need you, too."

If Chloe were strong, she would shake Elle until she changed her mind. Nevertheless, she wasn't. She was only weak.

Elle was right; she did need her. Elle knowing that was the reason she wasn't going to get a fight out of Chloe.

Never would she forget what she had done to Elle in the past, and now she was never, ever going to forgive herself for what was going to happen to Elle in the future.

I can honestly, truly say I hate myself and forever will.

The day seemed to drag by, and despite Elle taking the exact same schedule as her, they hadn't said a word to each other. Chloe was too upset to. She knew what this was going to mean for her best friend, and she was heartbroken.

When the lunch bell rang, they went through the shortest line of sloppy Joes. Elle got to the lunch lady first, giving her the lunch number.

"You have a balance from last year on your account. You need to get that paid if you plan to eat next week. Now move along." The lunch lady shooed her away, not wanting to give her the time of day.

Chloe was just as stunned as Elle with the lunch lady's attitude as she gave her own lunch number to the lady.

"You should transfer after this week, just to tick her off," Chloe told Elle as they took their seats at their table from last year.

Elle cracked a laugh before she shut her down. "As much as I would like to piss her off, that's not going to happen. I've made my choice, and I'm staying here."

"Well, then I hope you fail all of your classes."

"Aw, thanks, I appreciate that," Elle retorted as she held her hand over her heart.

She gave Elle a smile. "You're welcome."

They both laughed for a minute then began eating what no one else wanted.

"Who even hired a fifteen-year-old, anyway?"

"No one." Elle swallowed the food that was in her mouth. "A diner downtown hired a sixteen-year-old."

Chloe blinked her eyes a few times, digesting what she had just heard. "How in the world did you get away with that!"

"Easy. It's a crappy diner, and they needed a waitress so badly they hired me on the spot because a waitress had just quit. Put me to work that night and everything."

"What did your parents say?"

Elle took another bite of food, clearly trying to dodge the question before she finally gave in. "Well, they think I work at

Magical Cupcakes in the suburbs."

"Oh, my gosh." Chloe stared at her like she was a monster. "Do you just collect awards for all the lies you manage to pull off?"

Elle shrugged. "Possibly."

The two had missed each other a lot over the summer and were glad to catch up and be in each other's presence again. Chloe had spent the night over at Elle's a couple of times, but not as much as they would have liked due to her parents.

Stopping mid-bite, Elle's mouth almost dropped to the floor. "Oh, my gosh, who is that?"

Glancing behind her, Chloe saw an extremely tall and very well built teenage boy walking across the cafeteria before she quickly turned her head back around. "I don't know. Maybe he's a transfer. He looks like a senior."

She continued to gawk at him before her eyes got big. "No freaking way. Look! I think that's Amo!"

"What? No, it's n—" She stopped mid-sentence when she looked back to see him sitting in the exact same spot Amo had last year—at the table where his best friends Vincent and Nero sat. Vincent was the pretty blond, but Nero was like their group leader and perfection with his dark hair and skin along with his piercing green eyes. He and Vincent had managed to have every girl drooling after them last year, while Amo had been just a normal, awkward teenager. But now he was unrecognizable.

Elle had yet to move her eyes from him, much like all the other girls in the cafeteria.

"Jeez, it looks like he started eating roids for breakfast."

Chloe practically laughed up her sandwich. *I bet he's going to give Nero and Vincent a run for their money now.*

"Dang, he went from about a three or four to a solid ten really quickly."

Definitely a run for their money.

"Don't you think so?" Elle asked, still not moving her eyes from Amo once.

Chloe shrugged. "Eh, he's all right."

Elle finally moved her gaze to Chloe like she had been struck. "All right! Excuse me?"

"I think Nero is better looking in my opinion," she told her matter-of-factly.

Elle busted out in laughter. "Too bad his ego is about as big as Amo, which makes Nero a zero out of ten."

"We were ranking looks, not personality. If we were ranking personality, then they would all be zeros, and Vincent would round it out at negative one."

"What's wrong with Amo's personality? He's never really done anything."

He has to me... But Chloe decided to keep that information to herself.

"And that was pre-pubescent Amo. Puberty Amo will be a jerk like them. I mean, come on, he looks scary now." Chloe turned her head back to stare at him for a moment. "Like a beast."

When the nightmare ended and Chloe came to, she found herself clutching the jacket around her arms in desperation. Quickly, she went to wipe away the tears that had escaped during her episode, but there weren't any. It was only her imagination. Tears hadn't crossed her face in years. However, she could still feel them pouring out of her eyes and down her face from that night as if they were real. Now they were nothing but ghost tears.

With her eyelids growing heavier by the second, she lay down on her bed. It wasn't until she snuggled up to the fabric and inhaled Amo's scent that she realized she was using his jacket like it was her blanket. Not only that, but she had yet to let go of Amo's jacket from the moment he had draped it over her shoulders earlier that night.

Pulling it tightly around her, she had a strange feeling come over her that she couldn't understand nor realize what it was. It was something she hadn't felt in a long time because it wasn't of an evil nature. It was a feeling of contentment, of safety and security, making her feel like she could sleep … for once without the nightmares … without the devil haunting her …

    … just… sleep, feeling…

    …

    …

    …

    lov—

GOING BACK ONE MORE TIME

SENIOR YEAR

Chloe *hadn't gotten an ounce* of sleep the night before, and looking at her refection in the mirror, she could tell. Her gray eyes looked exhausted, and her skin was even paler than usual. To put it simply, she looked rough, and she highly doubted makeup was going to help. She was beginning to feel sick in the stomach, thinking about going back one more time to school.

After going through it for three and half years, you would think it had gotten easier, but it hadn't. Hearing the word "freak" still felt as hurtful as it had the first time she had heard it come out of Cassandra's mouth. The only reason she had survived this long was because of Elle, and she knew it.

Chloe still had yet to forgive herself that Elle still attended Legacy Prep High because of her. In fact, she still hated herself for it to this day.

It had gotten only worse for Elle since she had decided to stay. Some of the students had found out she worked at the diner, and since then, she was "gifted" the new name of "waitress." Cassandra and Sebastian had had a field day when they'd found out and had even gone to her work just so she could serve them while they treated her like garbage.

Many times, Chloe had begged Elle to leave and just forget about her, but she couldn't ever get her to. Chloe was trapped, and sometimes, she would wonder if it were all worth it, but Elle would never let her give up. Consequently, every day, she would get up and face her demons alongside Elle.

We're so close. There was no giving up now. They had only one semester left of high school, and today was their first day back from Christmas break. Just one semester was between them and college. Chloe was going to a college as far away as possible, and she hoped Elle was going with her.

She had nothing here for her, and she wanted to put her family, the people and place of Kansas City behind her.

Chloe stared at her refection, looking at the deep scar that she still carried. *Forever.*

If she and Elle could keep their heads down for just one final semester, then they might just make it out of the hellhole alive.

Looking at Elle's food all over the cafeteria floor had her frozen in place.

"Go on, clean it up, waitress," Cassandra told Elle after she had pushed Elle's food off the table.

The cafeteria had gone quiet, everyone wondering what Elle would do. Chloe wondered how Elle would respond, as well, but she didn't respond. Instead, it was like she ignored Cassandra.

Panic started setting in, and Chloe began to realize this was not going to end well.

"Bitch, I know you hear me."

She tried to move out of the way when Cassandra grabbed her plate and held it above her head, but Cassandra's two carbon copy best friends came to stand on both sides of her. Chloe sat back down instantly from the fear of them touching her to force her back down.

Cassandra's high voice rang in her ear, "Clean up the mess like a waitress is supposed to do, or the little freak will have her own mess to clean up."

Chloe began wringing her hands, making her nails dig deep into her palms, always wishing for the pain to help get rid of the terror.

When Sebastian hit Elle in the face with a washrag, Elle glanced at Chloe before she started cleaning up the mess. It took a lot for her to get on the ground in front of the whole cafeteria to clean it up, but she had been backed into a corner and just wanted to get Chloe out without any harm coming to her.

Elle cleaned it quickly, not wasting any time.

"Come on, Chloe. Let's go."

Seeing Elle's outreached hand was what got her to stop wringing her hands.

"Sorry, you missed a spot." Cassandra started to tip the plate over Chloe's head.

Without even thinking, Elle hit the plate as fast as she could, the contents covering Cassandra.

A loud screech came out at the top of her lungs as the students either busted out in laughter or stayed quiet in complete and utter shock.

"You fucking bitch! You are done."

The blood in Chloe's veins went cold, and her body began to brace itself for the storm to come.

When she felt the tug on her shirt from Elle, it snapped her out of it enough to run straight for the door.

Getting to the doorway, they found it blocked by their first period English teacher, Mr. Evans.

That was it for them. There was nowhere to hide, and there was no way ou—

"Elle, Chloe, go on back to class," Mr. Evans said with eerie calmness.

Not wasting a single moment, they scurried out, hearing Mr. Evans's voice trail off as they left.

"Ms. Ross, clean up the mess you just made. I can't have other students thinking they can get away with this, now can I? Oh, and when you're done, meet me in the Vice Principal's off ..."

So many thoughts began to swirl through Chloe's head as they headed toward their Spanish classroom. Never had Cassandra been challenged like that, let alone embarrassed by the whole school.

There is no way we are surviving after that. She won't let us.

"I am so sorry, Chloe. It was just a reaction. I didn't want her to spill it on you," Elle told her when they'd reached the safety of the classroom.

It was hard for her to catch her breath from just thinking about the plans Cassandra was going to have for them.

"I know, but what are we going to do? She is going to kill us. You know that."

"I have no clue. Any suggestions?" Elle asked her as she sat down and dropped her head on the desk.

"Yeah, we become high school dropouts."

Chloe couldn't believe how it all had gone to shit on the first day back. Everything they had gone through before with Cassandra was going to be child's play compared to now.

All she had wanted to do was keep their heads down so they could get out. *We were so close.*

ONE WORD: F.U.C.K.E.D

Chloe sat in the back of her class, alone and scared.

Unfortunately, the last class of the day, Elle and Chloe were separated, just like it had been for them freshman year. Except, this time, Chloe was the one taking Health, and Elle was the one taking art. In fact, this last semester of senior year was taking a turn for the worst, and it was giving her déjà vu.

"Wait at your desk when the bell rings. I will be back to get you. I promise I will be the first one out in the hallway," Elle told her when she dropped her off at Health class.

Impending doom set over her.

"Um, okay, I won't move from my seat."

"Good. I will see you in a little bit."

"Be careful, Elle."

She hated this. She knew Elle sounded strong and usually was just as strong, but she could see it this time—the glimmer of fear in her eyes as she walked away from her, in a hurry to get to her class. Chloe just hoped she would make it back to her unscathed.

Thinking back, Chloe could honestly say that freshman year had been the worst when it came to not only her life, but the bullying. Her scars had been the freshest then, and Cassandra had been trying anything to fit in to be at the top of the food chain. Yes, Elle had taken the brunt of it, and she didn't think she could take it again if it got as serious as it had the first time.

Or even as cruel …

Barely able to catch her breath, Chloe sat behind the lockers, clutching the scissors in her hands. Having no clue how it had gotten this far or even how she had gotten in this position, she just wanted to disappear.

It had all happened so fast when Cassandra had placed the scissors in her hands. She didn't even know why she had done it or what it had been for. Then, before she had known it, Cassandra had been fighting with some girl named Elle.

It all blacked out for her until she heard Cassandra's voice, "Chloe, give them to me."

Mustering up some courage, she concealed the scissors behind her back and planned to tell Cassandra that enough was enough. However, when she saw the scene before her, any courage she'd had quickly evaporated.

Elle was being held on the ground face down with Cassandra on top of her. With the help of her new friends, Stacy and Stephanie, holding her arms down, it wasn't much of struggle to keep her in place.

A trickle of blood started coming down Elle's face. By the looks of it, she had hit her head on the locker room bench on the way down.

Whatever she had been expecting from her best friend since kindergarten, it wasn't this. In fact, this was the first time she had witnessed anything like this from her.

"Chloe, give them to me," Cassandra repeated, sensing her reluctance.

Slowly, she revealed the scissors. Staring down at them, she was prepared to tell her no.

"You don't want to be like her, do you?"

Stunned was the only way to put it when those words came out of her mouth. And looking into Cassandra's eyes, Chloe believed her. Cassandra's eyes showed her how committed she was to being the most popular girl in school. It was almost as if she were daring Chloe to get in her way.

Frightened at what her best friend had become, Chloe shook her head and held the scissors out before Cassandra harshly grabbed them from her. Instant regret filled her when the metal no longer touched her skin, and she began praying Cassandra was only going to use them to frighten her.

"Now, bitch, think again next time you turn your back on me."

Chloe watched in shock as Cassandra took Elle's ponytail in her other hand and started cutting it off. Hearing Elle cry as Cassandra snipped away, the tears started to brim her own eyes.

What have I done? *was the only thing that went through her mind.*

"A girl like you doesn't need long, pretty hair like this, anyway," Cassandra told Elle as she waved Elle's own ponytail in her face.

Sitting up once they'd released her, Elle began to cry into her legs, holding them tightly in front of her.

Chloe could barely hold it together when Elle looked up at her with a now butchered haircut and tears.

"Sorry," she managed to get out quietly without breaking down with her.

Running out of the locker room to follow in her best friend's footsteps and leaving Elle there on the floor bawling like that was the hardest thing she had ever done at that point in her life.

I'm so sorry, Elle ...

Little had Chloe known, she was going to leave Elle in a much worse condition just a few short weeks later behind the school. She hated the part she had played that day, though, and she still apologized to her every time she noticed how long and pretty her strawberry blonde locks were getting. The length had been fully returned to her, and Chloe noticed how protective she had become over her hair, not even wanting a trim.

Cassandra was pure evil from that moment forward, along with her brother Sebastian, and after what had happened in the cafeteria, they were one word: F.U.C.K.E.D.

Brrring.

Watching the students swiftly leave the classroom to go home for the day, she waited anxiously for Elle to return safely.

However, she wasn't expecting Mr. Evans to be the one to enter the classroom first.

Taking a seat at one of the desks in front of her, he seemed like he was almost careful about it.

Seeing him closer than she usually did, she could tell why almost every girl at the school was secretly in love with him. He certainly didn't look like any other teacher here with his short, kempt, dirty blond hair and beard. His eyes matched perfectly, seeming almost golden. Not to mention, he was clearly built under his well-dressed clothes.

"You're not running out the door to leave?" Mr. Evans asked, snapping her out of her thoughts.

"N-no, I-I-"

"Are you shaken up after what happened earlier?"

Oh, gosh. Chloe shoved her hands to her face, not wanting to talk about this with him. The last thing she wanted to do was run her mouth about Cassandra.

See, Mr. Evans was new this year and had no clue how this school worked yet. The Ross's practically owned this school, and the teachers all looked the other way when it came to them. As a result, talking about it with him was only going to bring more danger to her.

She needed to think of an out quickly.

Elle abruptly entered the room, concern apparent in her voice. "Chloe, are you okay?"

"Yes, I'm fine, El—" She looked up and her eyes grew as wide as her stomach. Elle had something stained all over her clothes. "Are you okay? What happened?" Standing up, she went over to her.

Elle glanced at Mr. Evans. "Um, I accidentally spilled paint on myself in Art. What are you all talking about?"

"I was just passing by and saw Chloe in here by herself, so I was making sure everything was okay. Usually, the kids are practically one foot out the door before the last bell even rings."

"Yeah, I know what you mean. She's my ride, and I just told her we would meet up in here," Elle told him as he walked up toward them.

"How come you met up here and not in your Art class? The Art class is all the way at the front of the school by the outside door," he asked curiously, but by his facial expression, it seemed like he already knew.

"I guess we didn't think about it like that. I'll see you in the morning, Mr. Evans. Come on, Chloe; I need to get ready for work."

Feeling very uncomfortable with where this conversation was going, she gladly followed Elle out.

When Mr. Evans decided to give parting words, Elle stopped to look at him.

"Elle, if you ever need to talk, you know where to find me. Try and be more careful in Art. Next time, it might not be paint that spills."

A chill touched Chloe's skin at his warning.

"Have a good night, Mr. Evans," Elle told him as they left the classroom for good this time.

She waited until they'd reached the outside to talk. "So, who spilled the paint? And dang, all over your outfit. That one was my favorite on you." It really was. The big white sweater and her light jeans really brought out her tan skin and big blue eyes.

Elle's closet was not only limited in quantity, but also quality. She got the majority of her clothes at the local Goodwill, but you wouldn't ever know. Only the students here did because the only thing that mattered to them was how expensive the clothes they wore were.

"One of Cassandra's sidekicks."

Immediately, she knew it was one of her carbon copies: Stephanie or Stacy. They had definitely replaced her as Cassandra's BFF. She noticed Stephanie cozied up to no one other than Nero of course.

"Which one? Her?"

They could hear Stephanie and Nero speaking as they reached the school parking lot.

"Nero, would you mind giving me a ride home? I rode with Cassandra this morning," Stephanie said overly sweetly as she leaned against his Cadillac.

Nero quickly looked her up and down, revealing what they expected to do. "No problem, babe. Leo, let's go!"

A cute dark blond boy ran over to his car. He was clearly a freshman and obviously Nero's little brother.

"Backseat, Leo," Nero told him before they all got in.

Finally, Elle answered her, seeming distracted by what was going on between the two. "No, the other one."

Stacy.

Unlocking the doors on the BMW her father had given her the moment she could drive, they started climbing in. The car was definitely more of a gift for her parents than her. They hated driving her anywhere and thought of her as a nuisance. The only reason it was a BMW was because her father was still mayor of the city, and he cared about his "image." Her parents weren't about to let their daughter drive around in a shitty car, despite the fact that they hated the sight of her.

"Elle, is something wrong? You're acting weird today." She was beginning to become concerned. They needed to keep their heads down, and Elle was doing the opposite.

"I'm fine, Chloe. I guess I'm just getting tired of this same shit every day." She seemed to have gotten more of an attitude, as well.

"Listen, Elle, you don't have to stay. You're free to go. If your parents found out how you're treated here, they wouldn't let you come ba—"

"I am not leaving you, Chloe. I've told you this a thousand times." She stared at Chloe dead in the eyes, letting her know she still wasn't changing her mind.

Averting her gaze, she looked at the steering wheel. "Well, we have survived this long by not getting into it with them. I am not like you, Elle."

"All right, Chloe. I won't fight back. I promise."

For some reason, even though Elle was a great liar, Chloe didn't fully believe her words, so she tried to get her to understand.

"Fighting back doesn't solve anything, Elle. You know that." Turning on the car, she began pulling out. *It only makes Cassandra kill you faster.*

There was going to be hell to pay tomorrow, and she and Elle were on the ticket.

I'LL MAKE YOU
REGRET THAT, DARLIN'

In one quick motion, he jammed the tip of the shovel into the freshly dug dirt hard enough so it stood straight up. Wiping the sweat off his brow with his bloodstained shirt, he was able to take a moment's break before he climbed out, using the pile of dirt he had expertly removed and placed to get out of the eight-by-nine-foot hole. After he got out and looked down at his masterpiece, he thought it definitely looked much different up here than it did down there.

Going over to the form wrapped in a dark sheet, he kicked it until it rolled over, falling into what seemed like an abyss. You could always hear when it hit the bottom from the loud thud, and it never failed to bring a smile to his face.

Pulling out his cigarettes and lighter from his dirt-covered jeans, he took a seat on the ledge before he put a cigarette between his teeth. The zippo came to life with a flick of his wrist, and he lit the end, taking a long, deep drag.

He knew he shouldn't take the time for a smoke break, but it was a graveyard, after all.

Halfway through his cigarette, his phone began vibrating, and even though he didn't recognize the number, he had a pretty good guess of who it was.

A sexy female voice came over the line. "Is this Lucca?"

Smiling, he exhaled the smoke that filled his mouth. "Yes, darlin', it is."

"What are you doing?" She giggled.

Getting up, Lucca knew the hot blonde he had given his number to earlier in the night was going to be easy. "Smoking," he answered, starting the easy climb down from his pile of dirt. "And wondering when you were going to decide to call me."

She pretended to sound shocked by his answer. "I guess you're not busy, then?"

At the bottom again, he could see the form he had tossed in earlier. The sheet had revealed a cold, bloody face that had a bullet right between his eyes. "Not at all."

"Can I meet you in an hour, then?"

Lucca inhaled, making the cigarette illuminate his rugged appearance. "That depends on how hard you like to be fucked."

The phone went dead silent before her voice came back, practically moaning, "As hard as you can give."

"I'll make you regret that, darlin'," he warned her.

If she hadn't been moaning before, she was definitely doing it now. "No, you won't."

"One hour," he told her before killing the call. It was going to be a bit longer than an hour before he could get to her, but making her wait for him was half the fun. Giving her a warning that she was going to regret that statement was about the nicest thing he had done all day, and he was going to live up to his promise.

Flicking his bud on the dead body, he looked down at the man no one was ever going to see again. Any family or friends he left behind would never get closure.

"Fucker."

Lucca couldn't care less. The man had gotten what was coming. The only thing that upset him was the fact that he had let the man almost bite his hand off.

They had wanted to keep him alive to question him, but when Lucca had let go from the bite, his boss had shot him right between the eyes.

Getting back to the matter at hand, he picked the shovel back up and began transferring the pile of dirt back into its place. With each sling of dirt, more and more of the body was covered until the man no longer existed on this earth.

Lucca took pride in leveling out the dirt to make it flat once again. The hole was six feet deep exactly when he threw the shovel up and out of it. Though he no longer had his nice incline of dirt to help him get out, it wasn't hard for him to take a running jump out of it with his six-foot-three stature.

Now looking down at it from up here, you wouldn't even know he had disturbed the open grave or that there was already a man laid to rest.

By tomorrow, a Mary Johnson would be lowered in, according to the already placed grave marker, and the dirt would seal not only her, but the asshole beneath her.

"Mr. Johnson, you'll meet Mrs. Johnson tomorrow."

Picking up his stuff, he admired his work one final time. It was scary how good he had gotten at this now.

Good-bye, Mr. Johnson. I'll bring you more friends soon.

I'M GONNA PASS.
I'M NOT INTO DICK

*P*arking *his car behind Nero's* and Vincent's on the street, he got out, wondering why Nero had dragged them to Stephanie's house late at night.

"Did you take long enough to fucking get here, Amo?" Nero asked him.

"Listen, if we're here to have a foursome with Stephanie, I'm gonna pass. I'm not into dick," Amo retorted.

"The last thing I would want to see is your dick. Besides, you don't have to worry"—Nero flashed a smile—"I already took care of Stephanie, and even though I just dropped her off, I'm sure she's already passed out."

Vincent flashed his own smile. "I bet I could wake her up."

"For fuck's sake." Amo was on the verge of a headache. "Can you just tell me why I'm here? Then you two can go back to sucking your own dicks."

Nero's face turned dark, getting serious. "There was a murder tonight."

Blankly staring at him for a moment, Vincent still wanted to know why he was here. "Okay …?"

"Who gives a shit?" Amo was clearly as unimpressed as Vincent. Their fathers all worked in the same line, and killing sometimes just came with the territory.

"Well, my father just gave me my first job." That piece of information from Nero certainly made them give a shit. "And when I finish it, I'll be in."

Now he knew why they were there. "Can we get in on it?"

"I don't know yet. It depends on how difficult sh—the job gets."

"You can't tell us what the job is?" Vincent asked.

Nero shook his head. "Not yet. Just wanted to give you guys a heads up."

Amo and Vincent nodded their heads in understanding before they all went back to their cars.

Getting back into his car, Amo felt his blood start to pump. He was closer than ever to following in his father's footsteps. It was a day he had been dreaming of for as long as he could remember.

The day I become a made man.

"This is the best day of my life!" Chloe almost couldn't believe it when those words passed her lips as they headed toward the cafeteria. It was the first time ever Cassandra hadn't come to school, and not one person had said anything to them. She hadn't heard "freak" or "waitress" all day.

Elle chuckled. "I know. Best freaking day ever. I wonder why Cassandra isn't here."

"Who cares? I never thought one person was the sole reason for high school being such a nightmare for us." She had thought it was more like Cassandra, Sebastian, Stacy, and Stephanie, plus all the people who wanted to impress them by making fun of her and Elle.

"Yeah, me, either."

However, they still weren't stupid, so they reached the cafeteria and got food from the shortest line.

"I have to tell you what happened when you left me this morning. By the way, what the hell? Why did you do that?" Elle asked once they sat down to eat their lunch.

It took her a second to realize what she was even talking about, but then it came to her.

In their first period English class, Elle hadn't seemed like she was even there. It had seemed like something was wrong, or maybe something had happened, but she had snapped out of it pretty quickly when they had realized Cassandra wasn't going to be there today. Anyway, Mr. Evans had given them an assignment of writing a short, five-hundred-word essay the day before, and Elle hadn't turned anything in. Therefore, he had asked to talk with her after class, and that left Chloe getting to second period on her own.

"Because Mr. Evans said he needed to speak with you, not me. I knew it was about you not turning in your essay. He wasn't going to talk about it in front of me, you know that. Oh, and why didn't you turn in your essay? It was the first assignment of the semester."

"I was sick. Listen, I have to tell you something. You're not going to believe who talked to me and didn't want me dea—"

"You were sick? Really, that's the excuse you're giving me? I hope you didn't use that on him." She didn't believe that bologna for a second.

"Uh, yes, I was sick. That's the truth, and he believed me. Why can't you?"

"Probably because, not once have you *not* turned in an assignment, and you get sick all the time. You practically stay sick. There isn't anything that goes around that you don't catch."

Elle started to look like she was hiding something serious. She was the master at lies, so whatever it was, it must be bad for it to affect her to the point of not being able to pull off a lie.

"Well, this was a different kind of sick."

Oh, okay. Sure, a different kind of sick. What in the world is she hidin—

A male voice interrupted her thoughts. "Hey, babe, can I sit here?"

Chloe about choked on her food when she turned to see Nero with a tray. She thought she was seeing things—*wait … Did he just call Elle "babe"?*

Elle pointed to the empty seat beside her. "Are you serious? Sit *here*?"

"Yes, I was talking directly to you, wasn't I?"

Her mouth dropped to the table. The sarcasm was real in their voices, telling her that something must have happened between them. She was pretty sure of it by the way he was eyeing Elle. *Yep, he is, in fact, talking directly to you!*

Chloe was on the edge of her seat, wondering what Elle was going to say next.

"No, you clearly weren't because my name isn't 'babe.' I bet you don't even know my name. So, no, you cannot sit here, Nero."

Okay ... I wasn't expecting that.

"All right, babe. I'll eventually be sitting right there. I can wait." Nero left with a smirk on his face.

Okay, I wasn't expecting that, either. He definitely liked that answer more than he should have.

Chloe picked her jaw up off the ground and swallowed the food that was still in her mouth. "Don't you think I deserved a little warning?"

"Jesus, Chloe, I tried to tell you twice, but you kept interrupting me. I said you weren't going to believe who talked to me."

"Well, tell me already!"

"When you left me, I went in the hall, and he bumped into me. I tried to tell him sorry, but he told me to not apologize for something I didn't do. He actually talked to me and wasn't mean."

Chloe felt her mind being blown at this moment.

"I can't believe it. Nero is ... nice?"

"No way. He is ..." Elle drifted off. "He wants something, but I'm not going to find out what it is. I know exactly who Nero Caruso is, and 'nice' is the last word I would use to describe him."

"Yeah, but aren't you just a little curious?" Since today was a dream day free of Cassandra, she wondered how Elle didn't seem the least bit interested. "I know I am."

Chloe couldn't help it. She had always found Nero beyond handsome, and she could live vicariously through Elle. The way he had looked at her friend, with his piercing green eyes, had shown her something definitely was there, and if she could see it, then Elle should have definitely felt it. Chloe was the one who didn't like people around her.

"No, I'm not," Elle told her defiantly.

Well, that was the biggest lie if I ever heard one.

After that, the rest of the day went on rather quickly, and they found themselves back at Chloe's Health class for the last period of the day.

"Stay here and wait for me. We're not going to try to be bold just because Cassandra isn't here. Clearly she's the ringleader, but you know just as much as I do she is not the only one who likes to ruin our lives."

Chloe nodded her head. "I know. I'll wait right here."

"All right. Catch you later."

Going into the classroom, she took her seat in the back, hoping Elle would make it to class safely, even though they were having a great day so far. Like Elle had said, they weren't going to take any chances just because the witch of Legacy Prep wasn't there.

When class started, a strong feeling came over her. She couldn't quite place exactly what it was. Looking up from her desk, she glanced around the room, the feeling becoming more unsettling by the second.

Getting nervous, she started digging her nails into her palms. Focusing on her hands while she stared at them seemed to help. Slowly, the unnerving feeling began to dissipate... right up until the end of class when it returned to her full-force.

Quickly, she again glanced around the room, once more expecting to see the devil's eyes staring at her. When her eyes stopped roving, she found a different pair watching her, instead. They might not have been pure evil, but they were black as night.

Unable to hold the gaze for even a moment, she averted her eyes and went back to digging her nails into her palms.

Quit being silly, she tried to talk herself into having imagined it. No one had ever cared to look her way unless they were calling her a freak.

Feeling like she was just being paranoid, she looked back up at him, only to catch Amo blatantly still staring. It was harder for her to move her eyes this time, but thankfully, the school bell saved her.

Brrring.

Turning over her hands, she saw the little droplets of blood appear.

"You ready?" Elle appeared out of nowhere, seeming a bit disheveled.

"Yeah. You okay?"

"Uh, yes, why wouldn't I be? Okay, let's go!"

It was almost like it was in slow motion when Elle's hand reached out and almost grabbed hers. She had to look away from Elle and down at the floor as she pulled her hand up to her chest.

"I'm sorry, Chlo—"

"It's okay. Let's go." Chloe didn't wait for her to lead the way this time. Instead, she walked right past her and started the journey to her car.

That was the closest anyone had been to touching her in a long time, making her realize she was never going to be able to stand human contact. A thought had never been so sad to her until now.

Her hand felt like it had almost been burned by the close encounter, and she took a look at it to see the little red marks she had created from Amo staring at her.

Chloe had been right to call him a beast three years ago. *He just grew into it more and more each day.*

A DEAL WAS STRUCK

T he moment Sebastian stepped up to their lunch table the next day, you could see the rage radiating off him. "Have you heard why Cassandra isn't here?"

Even though his rage was directed at Elle, Chloe was too scared to breathe.

When Elle didn't answer, he only got angrier.

"Well, she was suspended. Do you know why?"

Again, Elle didn't even look at him.

Closing her eyes when his hands came up, Chloe's instinct was to think he was going to strike her—she expected it—but she didn't expect the sound when he hit the table, instead. It was so loud it caused pure silence in the cafeteria.

"I am talking to you, waitress!"

Elle finally looked at him, clearly terrified for her life.

"Now, do you know why?" Sebastian was losing it by the second. "Do you?"

It didn't matter that Chloe had kept her eyes closed, she could still feel it the moment he lunged for Elle.

"I better not see you lay your fucking hands on Elle, ever."

Immediately, Chloe opened her eyes to see Nero intervening.

"I don't want to see you talking to her or even looking in her direction, and that goes for Chloe, too. Because, if you do, I will make damn sure everyone in this school will be calling you the freak. Do you understand me?"

What? She looked just as shocked as Sebastian did.

Nero came off much more frightening than Sebastian ever did, confusing her about which one she should really fear.

After Sebastian nodded his head, he was released.

It didn't take Nero slamming his hands down on the table to command the student's attention.

"Their names are Elle and Chloe, and you will call them by their names."

She had to look at Elle to see if she had heard him correctly. Standing up for them to Sebastian was one thing, but sending a message to the whole school was something different altogether. This was Nero Caruso. He was practically the king here, and anything he said had everyone falling in line.

"You okay?" he asked Elle.

"Um, yeah, I'm fine."

The two girls continued to look at each other, trying to make sure this was real.

"Do you think I could sit here now?"

For the most part, Chloe was okay with Nero, and she could definitely deal with him for Elle. She knew something was for sure going on between the two, so him sitting with them one day wasn't going to bother her. She'd had to learn to deal with much worse from all the events her father had dragged her to through the years.

"Sure. Why not?" Elle smiled at him.

Yep, something is.

"Good." However, she wasn't expecting Nero to wave his friends over.

Her nerves started to set in. She wasn't going to be able to deal with them coming over.

"What are you doing?" Elle asked, moving closer to Chloe.

"Uh, I'm sitting here, and they sit where I sit," he said matter-of-factly.

"No, I said *you* can sit here. I didn't say they could."

"What's the big deal?" A second passed before he figured out why by the way Elle was blocking Chloe.

"They can't sit here, Nero."

Stopping his crew by just a motion of his hand, he said, "Ba-Elle, listen; letting them sit here will make sure no one will ever say or do anything to you and Chloe again. They won't hurt you. I promise. They won't touch Chloe, either. I give you my word."

She could see it on Elle's face when she looked at her that the last bit had sealed the deal.

Taking a seat beside Chloe, she gave him a warning, "You better not be lying to me, Nero."

Nero nodded for his crew to come over again, and with that, a deal was struck.

"It's going to be okay. I haven't let anyone in here hurt you, have I?" The words Elle whispered over to her were true. She had never let anyone touch her, always offering herself up for bait if it came to it.

This last semester was going to shit in a hand basket, and she knew Elle was only agreeing to it for protection. Therefore, she shook her head, letting Elle know she understood.

Please don't let him sit next to me. She held her breath when the biggest one came into view. For some reason, Amo scared her the most. She didn't know if it was his size or his dark eyes reminding her of ...

Her breath released when Leo was the one to take the seat beside her after Nero's guidance. Then Nero sat down on the other side of Elle while Amo and Vincent took the other remaining seats across.

"This is my little brother, Leo." Then he nodded at her. "Leo, this is Chloe."

"Hey, Chloe." For some reason, she didn't expect the young boy to extend his hand, taking her even more off guard with the strange situation.

Elle saved her, taking his hand, instead. "Sorry, she's germaphobic. I'm Elle."

The guys all stared her down at the word germaphobic, making her want to run away. You could tell they didn't believe it.

She didn't expect Leo to begin laughing. "That's freaking genius,

Nero. Why haven't we thought of that after all the gross hands we've had to shake?"

Thankfully, everyone joined in the laughter, and even she gave a chuckle. The conversation had taken a different turn than she'd thought it would. One thing was for sure: Leo had a lot of charisma for his age, and since he was a lot younger than her, Chloe felt strangely comfortable with him.

The more lunch continued on, the more comfortable she began to feel around them. For the most part, Elle and Leo were the ones to talk about how Leo was adjusting to high school. The other boys pretty much had quiet conversations to themselves, giving Chloe space to feel as if they weren't even there. She could almost block them out ... until she felt Amo's eyes lingering on her longer than she liked, and the more he did it, the more it started to irk her.

As Elle started to get up to take their trays to the trash, Nero stopped her, taking the tray. Then Amo came up to take hers, and she didn't know what possessed her to hold on tightly, not letting him take it. As a result, when he held on and pulled it slowly to him again, he easily won.

"I-I can throw away my own trash." Her eyes remained glued to the ground, unable to look at the beast with her outburst.

"Yeah, so what's your point?" Amo didn't wait for her reply, moving toward the trashcan. He knew she wasn't going to say shit back.

That—

"Catch you later, girls," Leo called out, already heading to his class.

Beast.

Something about Amo was extremely unlikable for her.

"What class are you in?"

"Spanish. Why?" Elle answered Nero's question.

Amo had already started walking out front before he even replied, "Because we're gonna walk you to class."

After he took Elle's arm to get her to start walking, it wasn't long before he stopped to look back at her. "What are you doing, Chloe?"

She had almost bumped into Elle's back from his abrupt stop. "Um, walking?"

"Why the hell are you walking on Elle's ass?"

Raising her right eyebrow that had a small patch missing from her scar, she didn't understand the point of his question. "This is how I always walk."

He ran his hands through his hair. "Jesus Christ. Chloe, walk beside Elle."

It was only when she noticed Amo and Vincent shaking their heads that she took a step to stand next to Elle. Then, when Elle nodded for her to go, she finally, reluctantly started walking.

The feeling of it was just weird. It was completely awkward for her to walk beside Elle. After growing used to looking at her back and being blocked by her, she felt like everyone was gaping at her as she walked past.

Looking up for a moment, she found out that they were, but for a different reason. They were gaping at the fact that Nero and his crew were actually walking with them.

By the time they reached their classroom, Chloe didn't waste any time before running in.

She had all but forgotten what it had been like when she used to walk beside Elle, and now that the memory was back, she decided, *I didn't like that, not at all.*

Leaning against the wall outside the back of the school with his arms crossed, he started shaking his head. None of this made sense.

"What are we doing here, Nero? Why do you suddenly give a shit about Elle and her friend?"

Nero shrugged, staring at the back of the school door. "Maybe I just want to fuck her."

"No, man, you don't try this hard for pussy."

Nero continued to just stare at the door, not answering him.

Amo looked at Vincent who wasn't getting what was happening, either. He started to head back to class. "All right, I'm out."

"Me, too." Vincent followed.

Nero waited until the door was about to close behind them. "Okay, fine."

The two came back outside and stood in front of him.

"What I'm about to show you, you didn't see." You could tell he was still contemplating showing them as he pulled out his phone and went through it. "I wasn't even supposed to take a video of it."

When Nero turned his phone around, Amo and Vincent glued their eyes to it. They thought it was just a picture of an alleyway at first, but then a strawberry blonde in an old timey diner uniform appeared with a trash bag in her hands.

Vincent looked up from the phone. "Is that Elle?"

"Yeah. Keep watching."

The video kept playing, showing Elle throwing the trash bag into the dumpster. You expected her to go back where she had come from, but instead, she ran to hide behind the dumpster where you could no longer see her.

"Shit," Amo said when Nero's father came into focus along with Nero's brother, Lucca, who was holding a squirming man. A man named Sal scoped out the alleyway, coming close to finding Elle before he disappeared.

They continued watching, knowing exactly what was going to happen.

The man trying to fight for his life looked like he had bitten Lucca's hand to free his mouth. Right before he could even scream, Nero's father shot him dead. They watched as a car then pulled up moments later, and the men all got in, escaping from what they thought no one had seen. However, right before the video ended, Elle reappeared, running for her life.

Vincent's mouth dropped open. "What the fuck? She didn't go to the cops?"

Nero shook his head.

No fucking way.

"This is bullshit. I don't believe it. That girl did not see anyone get murdered two days ago. She's acting too normal for that."

"That's why I took the video recording. I knew you wouldn't believe me. I didn't fucking believe it when I came to school yesterday, and that was after I saw the video." He put his phone back in his pocket after he clicked a few buttons. "I just deleted it."

The cat was already out of the bag, Vincent guessed.

"So what's the job?"

"She's still seventeen," Amo answered, figuring it out. If she were a year older, this conversation wouldn't be happening. The family would have killed her, no questions asked. "That means you've got to find out if she actually saw them and, if she did, whether she'll keep her mouth shut till she turns eighteen." *After that, she's as good as dead.*

When Nero nodded his head, affirming the job, he seemed conflicted or almost sad.

He likes her . . .

That was going to be difficult since the man who'd pulled the trigger was not only Nero's father, but was Dante Caruso, the boss of the Caruso mafia family. Then, to make it better, the man who had muzzled him was his brother, Lucca Caruso, the fucking underboss.

Amo went back to leaning against the wall. "If we help, then we get in, too."

"I'll make sure of it," Nero said, going back to staring at the door.

"I'm in," Vincent agreed.

When Sebastian appeared, looking high and mighty, Amo smiled. "This will be fun."

Nero was the one to move, and just how Sebastian had tried to lunge for Elle in the cafeteria, Nero lunged for Sebastian; except, he was successful in grabbing his collar to choke the shit out of him.

"I thought you were going to give me some fucking weed and apologize!" Sebastian choked out.

"Yes, and your dumbass believed it." Nero squeezed his neck harder until choking sounds started coming out of Sebastian's mouth. "I better not catch you trying to lay your fucking hands on her again."

Letting him go only for a second, Nero punched him so hard in the face he dropped to the ground, passing out cold.

Amo boomed with laughter that Sebastian could only take one shot to the face. He was pretty sure he had passed out more from fear than the actual hit.

Vincent frowned. "What the fuck, Nero? You took all the fun."

"Not all of it." Nero kicked Sebastian's helpless body before he swept his hair back into place.

Planting his own kick, Vincent kicked him in the ribs, giving him another bruise to wake up to.

Finally, Amo moved from leaning against the wall and went up to the still unconscious Sebastian. Even kicking him with only half his strength, it was still going to be the most painful one yet. Once his shoe made contact with Sebastian's balls, Sebastian woke up, screaming for just a second before he passed out again.

Amo's spit landed on the passed out boy's lifeless face. "Bitch."

HE'S CLEARLY A PSYCHOPATH

Chloe *wasn't expecting them to* be outside when their class ended. The look on Nero's face wasn't happy.

"What did I tell you?"

"You told me, but I decided not to listen."

Elle flashed a smile then went to take Chloe to her next class. Quickly, it evaporated when he grabbed her hand.

"Do you honestly think I should let you walk Chloe to class and then let you walk all the way by yourself to Art? I'm sure Sebastian is dying to get his hands on you … alone. But how about when they get smart and realize you don't give a shit what they do to you, and they go for Chloe? Cassandra is only suspended, but she will be back, Elle. And until then, Sebastian will do her dirty work, and so will Stephanie and Stacy."

"Yeah, you would know about Cassandra and Stephanie; you all are so close. Oh, wait, I forgot, Stacy, too."

"That is a separate conversation we can talk about later. Right now, I'm asking you, do you want to get Chloe hurt? Because you know I'm right."

It didn't matter if they were going to make her walk beside Elle, whether she liked them or not, or anything else. For years, her best friend had been her bodyguard because Chloe was weak, and now, though they scared the piss out of her, to be honest, she had to make Elle do it. Elle deserved better, and if they only did it for a day, then that was one day she wasn't going to get beaten up.

"He's right, Elle."

Sighing, Elle finally agreed. "Fine, let's go."

Nero kept Elle from walking. "We're going to do things my way now. Amo is in Health class with Chloe, so he is going to take her to class and bring her back to you in Art. Got it?"

Slowly, she started regretting her comment.

Elle shook her head. "No freaking way."

"This isn't a discussion anymore, Elle. Chloe, is he in your class?"

Looking at the floor, she wished she could lie. "Um, yes."

"Good. Now, Amo will take you to and from class for now. Only for the last class of the day, and he will sit beside you in class. Are you okay with that?"

No, I'm not.

Elle looked at her. "No, she's not."

When she looked back at her, Chloe could see they were both scared deep down of what could happen if they didn't take their help.

Chloe had to look away from her to say the word, "Y-Yeah."

"All right. Go on, Chloe. You'll be safe with Amo." It sounded like a genuine promise in Nero's voice.

"Come on, Chloe." Amo immediately started to walk away.

It took a lot for her to follow him, leaving Elle behind. On the outside, she hoped she looked strong to her. On the inside, she wasn't. Only the thought of her and Elle surviving this semester got her to move her feet.

Since Amo seemed to like walking out in front, she kept at his back, keeping a little bit more distance than she usually did with Elle. It certainly felt awkward. He was just so … huge. She could actually look at his back and wasn't able to even see what was on the other side.

Everyone seemed to move out of his way as he walked down the middle, not once moving an inch to the sides. She was only able to see anyone when they passed, and they certainly kept their distance from him.

Taking just a step closer to his back, she thought she might be able to get used to it. He certainly had a build for a bodyguard, and no one even noticed she was behind him since she was as short as most of the freshmen.

Reaching the classroom, Amo opened the door. She expected him to go in first, but he didn't. He waited for her to go in. Seeing how close she would have to get to him in order to pass, she waited for him to go in, instead.

"Go," he said harshly, clearly making no attempt for him to go in first.

I almost forgot he was a beast. Chloe passed him carefully, stomping into the classroom.

Amo let the door close behind him as he shook his head at her.

The whispering swirled in the classroom when they entered together, bringing her almost to a halt. It wasn't until Amo was about to run into her if she didn't move that she headed to her seat in the back.

Letting her long, black hair veil her face, she tried not to listen to the gossip of what had happened during lunch.

The tables in the Health class were set up a lot like the Science classroom with several tables that only held two people. Chloe's table at the very back actually only held one chair, but that was because no one really ever sat there, and the room was a chair short.

Finally reaching her chair, she began wringing her hands, the attention on her giving her anxiety. However, she was thankful to put distance between them. She didn't expect him to *actually* sit next to her like Nero had said. *Plus, there's no chair bes—*

A very loud and very obnoxious sound filled the room as Amo grabbed his empty chair at his old table and dragged it behind him, letting the legs scrape the floor.

Please stop. Please stop. Her embarrassment only continued until he placed the chair beside her at the table.

Smiling proudly, he took his seat. "You thought I wasn't going to actually sit beside you, didn't you?"

Chloe's answer was scooting her chair over to the very edge, though it didn't give her much more room because he practically took up the whole table.

By his smirk disappearing, she could tell he didn't like her answer very much.

It didn't dawn on her until class started how close she was to him. The only person she had ever sat beside was Elle, and now she was sitting beside the biggest guy in school.

Feeling the closeness between them, she went back to twisting her hands under the table, trying her best to concentrate on the lesson or anything that wasn't him. Amo made that rather hard. He seemed to like that she found him uncomfortable. Every now and then, he would remind her of his presence by adjusting in his chair, moving his arms just close enough for her hairs to rise on the back of her neck.

She didn't think the final school bell was ever going to ring. This was the slowest class of her life. Watching the clock slowly tick by, she practically jumped up a moment before the bell even rang.

Screw this. Chloe decided to take her chances with running to Elle rather than spending another second with him.

"I wouldn't do that." Amo's voice stopped her before she could even make a run for it. "Sebastian's locker is right outside that door, but if you prefer to take your chances with him, then be my guest."

Swallowing hard, she contemplated her options before she decided to stick with the lesser of the two evils.

Taking his sweet time, he waited until most of the class had left before he even got out of his seat to leave.

Falling in line behind him, she was finally able to glare at the unbelievable jerk's back, keeping her distance at first. It wasn't until they past Sebastian's death stare that she picked up speed to walk as close as she could to his back. *Wait . . . Is something wrong with his face?*

"Walk beside me," Amo growled over his shoulder when her feet hit the back of his heels.

Preferring to stay behind him, she decided to put more space between them, instead.

Amo stopped abruptly, wanting her to run into him to teach her a lesson. It only made him angrier when she didn't.

"Why won't you walk beside me like I asked?"

Chloe felt like a scared little deer in headlights, not knowing how to respond to his anger.

"I know you can talk, Chloe." Crossing his arms over his chest made him look even more intimidating. "Now answer me."

I-I—

She couldn't. She could only stand there, frozen, while she looked at the ground, hoping this would end.

Another low growl escaped his throat before he gave up in defeat, walking to the Art class without a response from her.

Continuing to follow him was hard, and the only reason she did was because of the look of death Sebastian had given her moments ago. Something had looked definitely wrong with his face . . .

Reaching the Art room, Chloe jumped out from behind him to see Elle, Nero, and Vincent.

"Nero, we need to talk. Chloe will not get off my ass. I told her"—Amo stopped midsentence to glare her down—"to walk beside me, but she refuses to even say a word to me."

That was it. She couldn't take him anymore. He clearly liked using his size to boss people around. She had called it years ago, saying nice Amo would turn into a jerky Amo once his puberty went to his head.

"T-that's how I walk!"

Elle laughed at her outburst.

"Oh, now you can talk because Elle's around. I blame you!" Amo directed his finger at Elle.

She stopped laughing. "Me? What did I do?"

"You taught her to walk like that."

Stepping up to him, Elle got in his face. "No, I didn't teach her shit. She learned to walk behind me when everyone started bullying us."

"We never bullied you."

"No, but you all sure as hell didn't stop it. Come on, Chloe; we're leaving."

Nero stopped her. "All right, calm down. You're right. We're just as guilty. All three of us are sorry, and we are trying to make it up from now on. But you and Chloe need to help us out here. Chloe, listen to Amo and try to talk to him every now and then."

No thank——

"And ..." Amo added.

"And get off Amo's ass. Walk beside him from now on. It's safer there, anyway. Someone could grab you from behind him if they wanted."

Swallowing, she thought back and realized Sebastian could have easily done that. Chloe nodded her head.

"Yeah, like she'll have much room to walk beside the beast." Elle stuck her tongue out at him.

Nero raised his hand when Amo looked prepared to smart back off to her. However, he walked off, heading to the school parking lot.

Her instinct was to still walk behind Elle, but Nero made her move. "Chloe, beside."

Walking beside Elle in defeat, she noticed Amo shake his head.

Once they got to the school parking lot, she could see Sebastian about to get in his car. That was when she realized what was wrong with his face. *How did he get a black eye?* It quickly became very obvious the guys had something to do with it by the look Sebastian gave them when he got in and slammed his door closed.

Amo began inspecting her car when he reached her BMW. "Someone slashed her fucking tires."

Yep, they definitely gave Sebastian the black eye after lunch.

Nero pushed his hair back, concerned. "All right. Elle and Chloe, I'll take you both home."

"It's okay. I've gotten flat tires before. I can drive on them for a few miles to the dealership." BMWs all came with special tires that allowed you to do that. She hadn't known until she had run over a nail and had to call her father for a tow. He had proceeded to tell her it would make it to the dealership before he had hung up on her.

Vincent couldn't help speaking out this time. "Oh, God, is she serious?"

"Chloe, you are not driving on flat tires, and not with Elle. I'll take you home. Your dad can take care of the car, right?"

She was afraid her father might get mad that she had left it. "I-I can drive it. That was the whole point of buying the tires."

Amo was close to running away. "Jesus Christ, I gotta get out of here. I'll take Leo home for you. Good luck with these crazies."

"Chloe, you're either going home with me and Elle, or Vincent will take you home."

Vincent flashed her his pretty boy smile at Nero's words.

Quickly, she changed her mind, blurting out her response, "I'll go with you and Elle."

That smile proved one thing. *He's clearly a psychopath.*

THAT GIRL NEEDED TO FIND ONE OF TWO THINGS: A NICE MOMMA'S BOY OR GOD

Chloe saw the *"good luck"* Elle mouthed to her as Nero drove off in front of her big, white house.

I'm gonna need it.

Sneaking into her house, she felt strange not going straight to her room. That was where she had learned to stay all day. It was safer there. The only time she ever came out was if her parents demanded her presence.

Trying to find her housekeeper Lana, she hoped to find her before anyone else.

Lana had been hired when her father had become mayor, and frankly, she was the best thing to come out of it. She was certainly more of a mother to her than her own mother ever had been, and Chloe could trust her with anything. Lana had cared for her since day one, picking up pretty quickly that her parents wouldn't win any awards.

A sigh of relief escaped her when she found Lana. She was sure to keep her voice down as she said, "Lana, I need your help."

"What's wrong?" Lana whispered back, concern showing on her face.

"My tires got slashed at school, and when someone offered me a ride home, they wouldn't take no for an answer. They said it would be too dangerous to drive it with all four tires out. I didn't want them to think—"

"Okay." Lana nodded her head understanding. "I'll tell them my husband drove your car to get fixed. I can drive you to and from school till then."

Relief flooded Chloe. "Thank you."

"Do you know who did it?"

Shaking her head, she could tell Lana didn't believe her for a second, but there was nothing she could do. Lana had questioned her parents in the beginning about Chloe, and they had told her, if she kept asking, they would easily replace her. Therefore, Lana had stayed on, keeping her mouth shut, figuring she could at least help Chloe in some way.

"Okay, go on upstairs. I'll bring your dinner up to you later."

"Thank you," Chloe told her again before quickly heading upstairs to her room. Thankfully, she made it without seeing her parents.

After setting her book bag on her bed, she quickly ran to her attached bathroom to relieve her bladder that she had held all day. Elle and she hadn't used the school's bathrooms once since becoming friends. The girls' bathroom was unmonitored, so the chances of them coming out alive were slim if they ever met Cassandra or any one of her friends. If it ever came to it, pissing yourself was a better option.

Once she was out of the bathroom, she took a seat on her bed, looking around her blank white room. The bed and nightstand were the only pieces of furniture present; nothing else was needed as she had a big closet to house her clothes, and her bathroom held her makeup and other girlie stuff. Chloe had never cared to decorate her room because this house wasn't a home, and her father broke anything she ever cared about. To her, it was just four walls and a place to lay her head at night.

Keeping the walls white made it easier for her to watch the nightmares play out, like a TV screen, then close her eyes to star in the show.

I know you can talk, Chloe.

Amo's voice entering her head froze her in place. She was used to hearing a voice in her head, but not that one.

Rinnng.

The ringing of her cell phone made her jump, scaring her half to death. Shaking off Amo's voice, she answered the phone, seeing it was Elle.

"Hey."

Elle didn't bother saying hi. "Did you tell your dad?"

"No. No point. I told Lana, and she said her husband will take care of it for me."

"That's good."

Chloe paused, not wanting to tell Elle about the fact that it meant Elle would have to ride the bus again until she got her car fixed. "Lana will be driving me till I get my car back, so ..."

Elle knew what she was getting at. "That's okay. Nero said he would give me a ride tomorrow morning, and I always have the bus."

"Oh, really?" Chloe smiled, thinking about her friend's new love interest. She could tell they were getting close pretty fast by the way he would hold her hand every chance he got.

For once, Elle was getting protection, so Chloe was definitely rooting for him, though his friends made her uncomfortable. That was something she was going to have to get used to if they planned to survive the semester.

"Tell me how the car ride home was."

"Fine."

Hmm. "Just fine?"

"Yep. Fine, Chloe."

Her mouth dropped to the floor. "He kissed you, didn't he?"

When the line remained silent, she knew she was right.

"Oh, he totally did! Tell me, how was your first kiss?"

"Well, it technically wasn't my first."

What! "Oh, my gosh, what?"

Elle didn't seem like she wanted to tell her the next part. "He kissed me earlier, in Art, in the supply closet."

I knew they were getting close fast.

"That is so freaking sweet."

"Yeah, yeah, yeah," Elle retorted. "Listen, Chloe, if you get to school before me, I can't help you."

She liked the other subject matter better, not wanting to think about getting to her first period by herself. "I know. I can figure out something, I guess. I'll be there at the exact time we always are."

"All right. I'll try to be there at the same time, but we know Nero is late practically every morning."

"I know." She hoped her voice sounded stronger than it was.

The pause over the line showed her it didn't.

"I'll see you tomorrow, then."

"Bye." Chloe went to hang up, knowing her friend not only needed to head to work, but wouldn't be able to say bye back.

The night was spent trying her best to keep busy with plenty of homework. The only break she took was when Lana brought dinner to her room, but after finishing it, she went straight back to her school work.

When her phone dinged later on, she read the text message from Elle.

Amo will be at school before you get there. Stay with him till I get there, okay?

No freaking way! She was happy her friend was concerned, but the last thing she wanted was for the beast to get more opportunities to walk her to class.

Quickly, she typed Elle a message back. **Please, no, Elle. I'll be fine.**

Chewing on her nails, she waited anxiously for her reply. Finally, when her phone dinged again, she read the message. **Cassandra could** be back tomorrow. Amo will meet you at your parking spot, all right? You know it's the best thing.

Dang it! She hated when Elle was right like that.

She typed in her regretful answer and hit send.

UGHH FINE!!

Falling back on the bed, she tried her best not to think about tomorrow. She slowly started drifting ...

You thought I wasn't going to actually sit beside you, didn't you?

Chloe shot her eyes open, expecting to see the beast, but no one was there.

Shivering, she remembered how close his arms had come to touching her during class ...

She shook her head, trying to keep the thoughts of him away.

Too afraid to close her eyes again, she stared at the ceiling where a pair of black depths flashed before her. At first, she could tell they were Amo's because they had a sort of sparkle to them. They were black, but not so black the person didn't have a soul.

Then the pair slowly became darker, growing abnormally large. These eyes had no soul behind them. Only evil lived behind those depths.

Unable to stare into the wicked eyes a moment longer, she had only closed her eyes for a second before the whisper of hands gripped her wrists.

Fighting to open her eyes again, she didn't have much time until—

Stay still, little girl, he whispered to her, *or it'll just hurt worse.*

It was too late; the devil had come for her.

Getting to school early the next morning, Amo hadn't expected to see Chloe's car still there. He had thought her father would have taken care of it ASAP, not wanting to leave a BMW sitting in a parking lot.

Exhausted, he leaned on the hood, rubbing his eyes. *So fucking tired.*

Yesterday had left him stressed out of his mind from dealing with those ridiculous girls. One in particular had crawled deep under his skin. Therefore, he had decided to call up Christa, a girl he had met who went to public school, to help calm his nerves. *And make me forget about that fucking crazy-assed Chloe.*

Needless to say, it hadn't really worked. Right when he had almost forgotten about her, Nero had called, interrupting his fun to tell him to be at the school early in the morning to babysit Chloe.

Several different feelings of dislike arose again, and Amo couldn't help thinking it was a bunch of bullshit that he was getting the shitty end of the job. Nero looked like he was off playing the fucking hero with Elle, and the likelihood that he was going to get laid out of it was pretty high. Amo, on the other hand, had to deal with her best friend who clearly had too many problems to count on one hand, just so Nero could stick his hand down Elle's panties.

Dammit, that fucker made me the damn babysitter, didn't he?

Well, he wanted to know why in the hell Vincent hadn't been nominated. He loved watching girls, and the more damaged, the better it was to him.

That was it. He was getting pretty boy to watch her.

Amo didn't like the way Chloe made him feel. He felt like he had done nothing except constantly think about her since he had stared at her in Health class just a few short days ago. The only reason he had looked at her was because Nero had gone over to their lunch table, and Amo had been trying to figure out why he had gone up to them in the first place.

After he had taken one look, he had kept going back for more glances without even realizing it. Never had a girl brought up such strong feelings in him, whether they were good or bad. Whatever they were now, he wasn't going to figure it out.

That girl needed to find one of two things: a nice momma's boy or God. The last thing she needed was a made man.

Noticing Chloe nervously coming up to him now, he believed she thought he was the devil. It looked like she was about to pull the fucking skin off her hands. He realized the only thing that could possibly help that girl was... *the Father, the Son, and the Holy Spirit.*

VINCENT COULD TURN A NUN INTO A WHORE

The moment she saw him leaning against the car, waiting for her, she wanted to retreat. She instantly regretted telling Elle she would let Amo walk her to class.

When she looked up from her hands, she came to a sudden stop from his stare. Amo looked at her like she was even crazier.

"It's way too early for this shit," he mumbled, passing her to begin walking to class.

That comment brought her back to remembering the jerk he was. Then again, despite being a jerk, he had yet to hurt her. Consequently, it was wrong for her to think he would hurt her the moment she looked at him. It was just ingrained.

Having to catch up with him at this point, she went to follow him. *Maybe I'm being too hard on hi—*

"Beside me," he growled at her when she got to his back.

No, I'm not.

Taking a small step, she strode to the side of him yet still stayed behind him in a way. At least it was to the side of him and not on his ass like he hated.

Rolling his eyes, he went to place his arm on her shoulder to help direct her. "No, besid—"

Fear gripped her as his hand inched closer, making her freeze in place. She dropped her mouth to scream at him to stop, but nothing left her mouth.

Instantly, Amo froze before he made any contact, seeing the pure fear that masked her face. A glimpse of worry appeared in his own expression.

"I didn't mean—"

Breathing heavily, Chloe felt like her heart was about to come out of her chest. For some reason, Amo scared her more than anyone had in a long time when there was no reason for her to fear him that way.

Whatever had appeared on his face quickly evaporated. For a split second, she had thought he might actually apologize.

"Just walk *directly* beside me." Again, he walked off, turning away from her.

It's okay. The beast didn't touch you.

Trying to make herself calm down, she went to follow him again before she made an even bigger fool of herself. This time, she walked *directly beside* him like he had demanded. All he had needed to do was tell her to do that in the first place. He didn't have to show her.

They didn't say anything else to each other as they continued to walk until they arrived at her English classroom.

While she went in and took her seat, Amo stayed outside. It was more than obvious they both didn't care for the arrangement.

That's it! I can't take him anymore!

When Nero and Elle approached Amo in the hallway, he could tell Elle was antsy as she looked inside to see if Chloe was there safely.

He wished he could tell Elle, *she's lucky I didn't spank her as—*

Amo was shocked when Elle hugged his side, taking his train of thought away. Then he practically shit himself as Elle managed to reach up and kiss him on the cheek.

"Thanks," she said, practically skipping away into the classroom.

What the fuck?

"Did she just do what I just think she did?"

Nero looked pissed. "Yep, she did."

"Hey, man, I didn't do anything." Amo held up his hands.

Nero took Amo's shoulder rather roughly. "It's fine, man. Someone looks like shit today. Rough night?"

Amo tried to keep his voice down, feeling quite passionate about this subject. "Try rough fucking morning. That girl is fucking nuts. I can't babysit her anymore. Tell Vince to do it; he'll like watching her."

"That's exactly why he can't watch her. Elle ain't going to trust him with her."

Dammit. Nero was right. Amo wouldn't even trust his grandmother with pretty boy. Hell, Vincent could turn a nun into a whore, but Amo had to keep trying.

"Well, I don't know what to tell you. She practically screamed when I almost touched her, and it wasn't the kind of scream I made Christa do last night."

Nero looked at him with a serious expression, trying to put things in perspective. "Listen, you know our job. We want in, don't we?"

Fucker.

He nodded. "Okay. Fine."

"Christa, huh?"

Nero had called him last night while he was with Christa, and he had asked about setting something up with her and her friends. Amo wasn't sure how serious he had been, considering Elle was in the picture. She was only supposed to be a job to Nero, but he thought there was more going on. *I guess I'm about to find out.*

"Yep, and Christa has a shit ton of friends waiting to meet some prep school guys tomorrow."

Nero answered quickly, "Good. You, me, and Vince deserve a reward after these two."

Amo thought he answered a little too quickly. *I bet she's giving him blue balls.* He wasn't quite sure if Nero even realized he was falling for the girl, but he wasn't about to tell him.

"Yes, we do, man."

The next part that came out of his mouth, he didn't know why it mattered, but it was bothering him.

"Oh, that reminds me. When I met Chloe this morning, her car was still there. I figured her dad would have picked it up."

"Yeah, me, too. Maybe he was too busy running the city." Nero seemed as confused as he was about it.

Glancing inside to see Chloe gossiping with Elle, he thought better of it. "Or maybe he doesn't like dealing with her crazy ass just as much as me."

"Elle, I can't deal with him. He's crazy!" Chloe whispered, not wanting Amo to possibly hear her. Regardless, it was hard when she felt so strongly.

"Shh, I know, but you are here in one piece, untouched, right?" Elle looked concerned that maybe someone had hurt her.

"Barely! He tried to push me to walk beside him. All he had to do was tell me to."

Elle laughed, clearly thankful that was all it was. "Chloe, you gotta start to get used to walking beside us. It's okay as long as we're with them. This is a good thing we got going now. I'm not as worried anymore. Are you?"

Dang it! Elle was right. She feared Amo when he had given her no reason so far, and Elle was getting protected. She was going to have to deal ... for now.

"No, I'm not that scared when they are around."

"See, Chloe. They can get us to survive the rest of the semester. Then, when we're out, we won't need them anymore."

"Whatever. Fine." She sighed, regretfully agreeing.

Elle tried to cheer her up. "Want to go shopping tomorrow? I got Friday off. I think we deserve it."

"We sure do ... surrounded by those three idiots."

THE SOUND OF SEBASTIAN PISSING HIMSELF

"**S**o, *what do you girls* want to eat?" Nero asked once they got in the lunchroom, unaware of what exactly that question meant to them.

Chloe looked at Elle, not knowing how to respond. And by the way Elle quickly dropped her hand from Nero's, she didn't know how to answer that question any better than her.

He then told them like they didn't already know, "It's either pizza or the same line that's always been here of chicken patties and hamburgers."

"I don't care."

"Yeah, uh, me, either." Chloe went back to staring at the floor.

"Jesus, pick already. I'm fucking starving." Amo was clearly still not in a better mood than he had been this morning.

"Chicken patties sound fine," Elle answered after seeing no one was really in that line.

Vincent didn't seem to approve of their choice. "Who the hell doesn't choose pizza?"

"Elle, do you like pizza?" Nero asked.

"Yes," she mumbled her response.

Amo crossed his arms over his chest. "Chloe, do you eat pizza?"

Not like you care, anyway. Chloe nodded only after she looked at Elle for approval.

"So, why the hell can't I have pizza?" Vincent asked.

"Elle, why did you pick that line?"

Don't answer. The looks on their faces were turning scary.

"We always pick the line that doesn't have anyone in it."

"And what happens if the lines are about the same?"

Elle, stop answering Nero's questions! She couldn't help wringing her hands, feeling the rage begin to radiate off them.

Leo popped up out of nowhere. "Hey, guys, what's up?"

"Shut up, Leo. Answer the fucking question, Elle!" Amo roared, clearly already knowing the answer but wanting to hear it.

Chloe dug her nails into her skin when she felt Amo's eyes move from Elle to her. *Why does he care all of a sudden?*

Elle stared at the ground, unable to meet their faces any longer. "If the lines are even, then we pick the line that has the least scary people in it."

"Jesus Christ," Nero voiced.

"For fuck's sake," Amo said more loudly.

"Motherfuckers," Vincent somehow responded the loudest.

Leo's eyes danced around the group. "Does that mean they don't want piz—"

"Shut up, Leo!" the boys all said as one, scaring Elle and Chloe.

"From now on, you fucking eat what you want to. Do you both understand?" Nero told them.

Elle was quick to nod her head.

Chloe kept quiet, still a little frightened of the scary trio.

"Chloe, if you want fucking pizza, you eat fucking pizza, got it?"

Her eyes grew wide when Amo bellowed, demanding an answer.

Fiercely, she nodded her head, not wanting to make him even madder. He had looked mad enough about it, and she didn't understand why.

The moment Elle took off for the pizza line, Chloe was right behind her. Hearing Vincent say, "Let's fucking kill 'em," made her scurry faster.

By the time they got in line, everyone was already there, so they were forced to be in the very back. Leo caught up to them first and was shortly followed by the three guys.

Chloe swallowed hard. *They look like they're ready to go on a murder spree.*

"No way I'm waiting this fucking long. You know they run out of pizza. Let's cut."

Elle stopped Amo. "No, that's wrong. We're not cutting."

"Sorry, sweetheart. After what you just told me, I frankly don't give a shit about right and wrong." Vincent started cutting up the line, yelling "move" to anyone who didn't do so at first.

Amo was quick to join in, and suddenly, the line parted for them. Nero shoved Elle to go, and Chloe was forced to follow.

Feeling extremely uncomfortable didn't even begin to describe how it felt for her to cut every student in line who had ever called her a freak. *Please let me dissap—*

When a tray was extended to her, she looked up to see Amo holding it out for her. It was the first time she could see something that almost seemed nice under his rough exterior.

Slowly, she took it from him, having to look away as she did. She had grown almost used to the roughness of him and seeing him differently for once seemed weird.

They all went through the line rather quickly and were at their table in no time. Sitting down, she could tell Elle got embarrassed when Nero kissed her on the cheek, but Chloe found it rather sweet. It was obvious the two were perfect for each other.

Getting nervous over who was going to sit beside her today, she was relieved when it was Leo again.

This day is turning out okay after all. Chloe almost smiled as she brought her pizza to her lips. Picking school lunches around everyone else sucked because they were never able to eat the good stuff.

Nero quickly took notice of the joy on their faces. "When was the last time you ate pizza at school?"

You could tell Elle was uncomfortable again. "Since middle school."

"I had it freshman year," Chloe chimed in, regretting her statement the moment it came out. The pizza was just so good compared to the chicken patties that she wasn't even thinking.

Again, the tenseness returned full-out, and the rage that had eased a bit came back in an instant.

Leo tried to ease the tension himself, voicing the question he'd probably had the second he had seen her scars. Since he was younger than them, he wouldn't know.

"Chloe, how did you get those scars?"

The table went silent, and the boys all waited to hear the words come out of her mouth.

That had been the first time in a long time anyone had asked her that. Everyone just knew and made fun of her for it. At least, everyone knew the lie her father had created.

As she stared down at her plate, the devil's eyes appeared before her, reminding her exactly how she had gotten them.

"She was in a car accident," Elle answered, seeing Chloe couldn't.

His mocking laughter rang in her ears. *Lies.*

That only made Leo want to know more.

"Oh, dang. When?"

Stay still, little girl . . .

Her heart began to race, knowing something was about to come.

"When we were freshmen." It was obvious Elle didn't like talking about it any more than Chloe.

. . . or it'll just hurt worse.

Chloe held her breath, waiting for impact.

Later that day, Amo began walking in the direction Sebastian was running.

"I'm going back to class," he told his friends, leaving them outside of the school.

He didn't know why the fuck Nero had let Sebastian off easy since the last conversation they'd had with him clearly hadn't been effective enough. He damn sure wasn't going to stand around and agree with Nero like Vincent had.

Today, Amo had found out just how badly Chloe and Elle were treated, and it had rattled something deep inside of him. All these years, they had gone to the same school, and they'd had no idea of just how bad it was.

I have no one but myself to blame.

Opening the back door to the school, he knew Sebastian was still on the other side of it. He was trying to catch his breath and wipe the tears away from his face. So, by the time Sebastian saw Amo, it was too late.

Amo covered his mouth to muffle the screams and shoved him up against the wall with as much force as he could. Staring down at him, he could see the fear grow tenfold in Sebastian's eyes.

"I don't know why Nero didn't beat the fucking shit out of you just now."

The tears the little bitch had just wiped away merely returned.

When Amo pushed his arm into his throat, Sebastian started choking into his hand.

"I should just fucking snap your neck right here."

When he finally heard the sound of Sebastian pissing himself, he let up the tiniest bit.

"But Nero won't let me, so if I find out you did have something to do with hitting Elle in the face at lunch, I will make damn sure Nero won't make the same mistake again." He pushed his arm harder into his neck, the smell of his piss greeting his nose. "But if I find out you ever laid a hand on Chloe, I *will* snap your fucking neck next time."

Once he let go of Sebastian before he did just that, Sebastian ran off, this time surely not to get caught again.

Amo tried to calm himself down from seeing that milk carton drill Elle in the face at lunch today to the point she bled. He was sure it had pissed Nero off just as much, but what he hadn't expect was the look in Chloe's eyes. She had sat there, unmoving after it had happened, clearly going through inner turmoil and completely and utterly afraid. Not once had he ever seen someone truly afraid until he had looked into her eyes. Whatever she had gone through, he wanted to know. And after today, he didn't believe she was in a car wreck. *Not for a fucking second.*

THE BEATS MIGHT NOT BE SO BAD AFTER ALL

"**A**ll right, *Amo. You can* take Chloe to class."

"What? No. We need to all walk together," Elle told Nero, not wanting to take a chance they would try something again just after they had tried to take her out during lunch.

Chloe wanted to agree with her friend, but Amo's voice spoke low, commanding, "Come on, Chloe."

Seeing Elle push at Nero's chest in disagreement, she realized how much she had truly held Elle back all these years. Like today, when her friend had gotten hit, she hadn't even moved to see if she was okay. Instead, she had been stuck in her own hell inside her head. It was time to start pulling away from Elle just a little so Elle could be free.

Having to look away from Elle, Chloe looked at the floor as she walked away with Amo.

She could hear the little fight Elle tried to put up, but Nero wasn't having it, keeping her in place. It was hard to walk away from her like that. *But I have to start cutting the cord a little . . . for her.*

Chloe fell in line behind Amo, causing him to quickly stop and turn around.

"Don't make me show you again . . ." His voice was so low it was like he was daring her.

Her eyes almost popped out of their sockets. She quickly moved directly beside him before he even finished his sentence. There was no doubt he was still furious from lunch, and she couldn't help wondering if someone might have suffered a terrible fate while they had been in their last half of Spanish. Last time, it had been obvious the boys had skipped the last half of their classes and gotten to Sebastian, giving him a black eye. Her instincts told her they had gone back for round two.

Walking beside him was exactly as terrible as you would think. Everyone—and I mean everyone—stared at them while giving them a wide berth. It was like the hallway had split, and everyone lined up against the lockers to watch them pass.

She was sure she had drawn blood in her palms with how hard she was pressing into them. *Please let it end!*

Getting closer to the classroom door, she couldn't take the stares anymore, so she made a run for it, and she had barely touched the doorknob before his voice boomed.

"Chloe!"

Suddenly, she dropped her hand.

Amo approached the door, opening it himself.

Why couldn't you just let me run away?

She felt even more embarrassed by the scene he had caused.

After walking into the classroom slowly, the door slammed behind her from Amo making even more of a spectacle. The room of students drilled their eyes into her even more than the ones had in the hall.

Finally making it to her seat, she scooted to the very edge of the table as Amo sat down beside her.

"Why did you just run for the door?" he demanded quietly.

She could feel the blood start to trickle down her nails at this point.

"Tell me why, Chloe," he demanded again.

She had yet to look at him, let alone give him an answer.

Staring at her, he finally noticed her twitching hands. "Open your hands." He could see the little bit of red peeking out under her fingers. "Chloe, open your damn hands before I open them myself."

Gently, she opened her hands, too afraid he would follow through on his threat. She didn't have to look at him to know what he was thinking. *Freak.*

"Fuck." Jumping up, he didn't waste time before going to the front of the class and grabbing the whole box of Kleenexes. Coming back, he ripped a bunch out. You could see he wanted to grab her hands and hold the tissues to the marks, but he didn't. Instead, he carefully laid them on her hands, making sure he didn't touch her.

The act was almost ... *sweet.* It made her wonder if he was even a beast or jerk at all.

Closing her hands, she let the tissues start to soak up the blood.

This time, his voice was soothing when he asked, "Why did you run for the door?"

She found out she could talk to this Amo. "E-Everyone w-was staring at us."

"Is that why you did this to yourself?"

Solemnly, she nodded her head.

Pulling out more tissues, he made her change them out. "Put more pressure on it."

She closed her hands more firmly to stop the bleeding.

"I'm sorry I yelled at you. I thought you were doing it just so I couldn't hold the door open for you again."

She was finally able to meet his dark eyes. To actually see how badly he really did feel about it made her heart twinge a bit. She wasn't sure if she really knew him at all. Finding out he had only made the scene because he had wanted to hold the door open for her was cute in a chivalrous way.

"It's o-okay. I'll let you hold the doors from now on."

He actually cracked a smile at her joke. It was the first one she had really seen on him.

Brrring.

She quickly averted her eyes. The bell had made her realize she was staring at him. Her cheeks flushed a bit when he didn't move his eyes off her right away.

Their class seemed to creep by, and about a third into it, Amo made her check her hands to see if the bleeding had stopped. It had, so at that point, Amo got up, uncaring of the teacher lecturing, and threw away all the used tissues, as well as placed the tissues back on the desk.

As he walked back to his seat, Chloe felt his stare until he sat down.

The remainder of the class, she felt herself get a little bit more comfortable next to him. It wasn't much, but a small difference was some kind of progress. This seemed to make the class go by faster, and when the last bell of the day rang, she was surprised for once.

"You're not gonna try to make a run for it again, are you?" he asked when she quickly got up.

"N-No, Sebastian's locker is out there, and you basically said you wouldn't help me, remember?"

A smug look crossed his face. Instantly, she forgot all the nice things Amo had just done for her.

"Y-you d-did something to him."

His face dropped. "No, I didn't. I went back to class. Nero and Vincent were the ones who went and saw him."

Chloe bit her lip, "Really?"

"Yep," Amo reassured her.

Staring at him for a moment, she began to believe him. *At least, I think he's telling the truth . . .*

Standing up, he went to the door then stopped when she didn't follow. "You coming?"

Chloe didn't want to feel the stares on her again.

Seeming to read her mind, Amo asked, "You know why they're staring like that, don't you?"

She looked to the floor. "Because they think I'm a fre—"

"No, you're not a freak," Amo snapped. He paused for just an instant before he said, "It's because they've never seen me walk a girl to class before."

She didn't believe him at first, but thinking back, she realized she hadn't, either. Nero and Vincent were always the ones with girls wrapped around them between classes.

Building up the small amount of courage she had inside of her, she took her first step toward the door. *The beast might not be so bad after all.*

Anger exploded out of Chloe as she stared at the beast. It was a feeling she hadn't felt this pure probably ever in her life. It only grew worse with each tear that fell down her friend's face. She had seen Elle get the shit beaten out of her, but she had never witnessed her in this much pain.

They had just caught Nero, Amo, and Vincent in a fight, but that wasn't the worst part. When girls in tight dresses had wrapped themselves around the boys, Chloe certainly hadn't been shocked Vincent accepted it or even Amo, but she had been shocked Nero had a girl wrapped around him. Chloe could see it in Nero's eyes every time he looked at Elle: he loved her. She didn't know why he would fuck all that up.

"Let's go," Elle told Chloe through the tears. She had basically just told Nero to go fuck himself and only wanted to get away from him.

The anger hit its reaching point inside of Chloe. *I thought we were all starting to be friends.*

Nero and Elle were what was holding the alliance together. Without them, there was no friendship, especially since he had done something like this to cause such heartache to her.

She knew exactly who had played the major part in this. *I can see it on his freaking face.*

Rearing back her foot, she kicked him in the shin as hard as she possibly could.

"Ow! What the fuck did I do?" Amo yelled, holding his shin.

"You should be ashamed of yourself." She then pointed at Vincent who started to back away from her, afraid of the safety of his own shin. "And you, too."

Looking back at Amo, she let him know she knew this had all happened because of him. "I know you put him up to this."

Walking over to her now crying and somewhat smiling friend, Chloe stopped and looked at Nero. "I have nothing to say to you. You know what you just lost."

With each step to her car, the anger slowly left her body, making her realize what she had just done. It was like ... *I was possessed.*

Getting in her car and seeing Elle in the passenger seat wiping away the tears, Chloe felt the need to cry hit her, too. If she could, she was almost certain she would cry right beside her.

Fear set into her, but it wasn't the kind she was used to. Back there, she had thought Elle was the one with the most to lose with Nero. However, she felt like she had lost something just as great. Every day, Amo surprised her; every day, she had trusted him a little bit more; and every day, she could feel the start of a friendship blooming.

The fact that she was feeling the start of a friendship with Amo scared her. The fact that a strong sadness came over her since she wasn't going to see their friendship bloom truly frightened her ...

Did she just fucking kick me? Amo's leg still stung as he walked to the car.

Damn, she did just fucking kick me!

She had blamed him for Nero going out with another girl, but the only reason Nero had gone out was because he really hadn't had much of a choice. He had set the date up before Nero had realized he fully wanted her. Amo knew Nero would come to the conclusion of picking Elle over the job. It was obvious he liked her too much. However, Nero had to pretend to the boss that he wasn't falling for her, because if the boss found out about them and then they canceled, it would look suspicious. Nero's father was already skeptical of his loyalties.

Cassandra had also been supposed to be here tonight. Since she had been suspended this week, they hadn't seen her. They wanted to talk to her outside of the school, force her to tell them all the shit they had done to Elle and Chloe.

Nero had planned to kill two birds with one stone tonight: gain his father's trust and get his hands on Cassandra. But it all had gone to fucking shit the moment Elle had showed up.

They didn't even understand why she had come to Poison, anyway. It was a lounge for teens and definitely not somewhere Elle or Chloe had ever gone before. Elle had said she had gotten a text from Nero to come here, but he hadn't sent one.

We're getting played somehow. Someone was one step ahead of them, and he could feel it. He just hoped it didn't come to bite him in the ass before he could see it coming.

You should be ashamed of yourself . . . Chloe's words swirled in his head. She could barely look him in the eyes day by day, yet tonight, she had stared the beast down and kicked him. He was used to seeing that hint of fear in her eyes every time she looked at him, but for the first time, he had seen it disappear for just a moment.

Fear was the only thing he had thought lived in Chloe. *But, damn, I was wrong.*

A smile touched his lips. No girl had ever dared to do something like that to him. Not only that, but he had let her live to tell the tale. Whatever he had done to change her image of him had worked. He hadn't seen it until now, but that was exactly what he had hoped for.

There was no doubt Nero was getting Elle back, which put him right back where he wanted.

Before he opened the door to his car, the clicking of heels came up behind him. "Amo, you didn't forget about me, did you?"

Turning around, he saw Christa perking her boobs out for him to stare at. Instead, he turned back around to get in his car. "No, I didn't."

"But-but, I thought I was going over to your house tonight."

Amo opened the door and slid in, ignoring her obnoxious baby voice and fake tears.

"How am I supposed to get home?"

"Walk." He slammed the door in her face.

Starting the car, he ignored the girl yelling profanities through his window and throwing a hissy fit. *I can be a nice boy.*

He revved his engine, pulling out and leaving behind the girl as she tried to throw her shoe at his car but miserably failed. *I can at least pretend to be.*

YIN AND YANG

t was rough for both of them when Monday came and Nero and Elle were still not talking to each other. It was even rougher considering Cassandra's suspension was now over. With Cassandra back, they had agreed to let Vincent walk them to class since he was the person they blamed the least, considering Vincent couldn't ever help himself. He was just nuts.

When Vincent and Elle dropped her off at Health, it was weird, because a part of her had kind of grown used to Amo taking her. *Nope. No, I didn't.*

Going in, she took her seat in the back and placed her book bag on top of the table beside her where Amo sat—well, used to sit. She was making sure he wasn't going to sit beside her now.

The door was flung open a minute later, making her hold her

breath when the beast entered.

She immediately dropped her eyes to the ground, afraid to look at him once he saw her bag taking up his seat.

As she felt him stalk closer and closer to the table, her resolve began to break little by little. It was obvious he had seen the bag by now, and it was obvious he didn't give a fuck about it.

Amo approached the table. "Are you trying to tell me you don't want me to sit here?"

Looking up at him was a bad idea.

Swallowing hard, she nodded her head to the best of her abilities.

"That hurts my feelings," he told her in a sad voice.

Chloe simply stared at him, stunned. She wanted to rub her eyes to see if this was even real.

"That's not fair. You are giving Vincent another chance."

She couldn't believe it. He genuinely looked sad.

"B-but, Elle gave him one, too."

"Well, I won't tell if you don't." Amo pushed her bag over and took a seat before she could even think about protesting.

Brrring.

Dang it!

Chloe scooted her seat all the way over to the end. With the class beginning, she didn't have a choice; she had to sit beside him.

Instinctively, she put her hands under the table to wring them.

"Place your hands on the table," he whispered over to her.

She quickly shook her head and started to press her nails into the skin.

"Please, Chloe. I can't take you doing that to yourself," he pleaded.

When she glanced at him, it was the first time she really looked at him, like *really* looked into his eyes. They weren't the black abyss staring back at her like she had always thought. They might have been dark, but they also had a lightness to them. Almost like a sparkle of silver running through, giving them life. They were dark yet light, reminding her of yin and yang.

Taking a breath, she placed her hands on the table.

Amo smiled. "Thank you."

She had to look away from him after the charming smile he had given her. *What in the world is going on?*

It was hard for her to keep her hands on the table, especially when all she wanted to do was wring them until she had no skin left.

About halfway through class, it just got worse when the sudden urge to pee hit her hard. She had always been careful about how much water she drank at school, but today, she had been so thirsty she was now paying the price.

Will this class never end? Chloe twisted in her chair, trying to be discreet. If he hadn't sat beside her today, she wouldn't have had to worry about the embarrassing movements that would catch his attention.

"What are you doing?" Amo asked, looking like he was also getting antsy from all her movements.

Instantly, she stopped moving, clenching her book in her hands. "N-nothing."

"Something's wrong, or you wouldn't be squirming like that."

Chloe just buried her head in the chapter Mrs. Saylor was

lecturing on. It was bad enough to have to sit and listen to the reproductive organs of a woman, but the full bladder made it nearly impossible to take notes.

"You going to tell me ... or do I have to figure it out myself?" The snicker in his voice had her knowing he already knew what was the cause of her distress. It was hard for her to refrain from kicking him again.

"I need to go to the restroom." She had been whispering before, but she whispered even lower this time.

"Then ask for the hall pass."

The last thing she was going to tell him was that she was afraid to go in there. "I-I can wait."

"I'm supposed to watch you for the next thirty minutes, instead of you just going to take a piss?" Unlike hers, Amo's voice was only getting higher.

Chloe wanted the floor to swallow her to hell. It would be easier than the stares she was getting from his loud voice. *Does he always have to make everything a freaking scene? Or does he just like embarrassing me?*

She whispered over to him somehow lower, "Please be quiet. You're going to get me in trouble."

The sigh that came out of him blew her hair across her cheek. She pushed it back to see him sitting straighter in his chair, *No please!*

"Mrs. Saylor, Chloe needs to go to the restroom."

What would he do if I picked up my book and hit the smirk off his face?

Mrs. Saylor went to her desk, picking up the card. "Don't take too long."

Chloe felt her mouth drop open and her face turn red. "Yes, Mrs. Saylor."

She rushed from the classroom, unable to breathe after closing the door behind her. She hadn't wanted any more attention drawn to her, yet the whole class had watched her leave, and she would have to go back inside to their stares. *Breathe . . . Breathe . . .*

Gripping the hall pass, she walked around the corner to the restroom, already dreading going back. She didn't stop to think before entering the kill zone.

Stacy and Stephanie were standing by the bathroom window, smoking a joint. *Oh, God. Oh, God. I'm going to die.*

They didn't move, watching her with their beady eyes.

"What the fuck are you doing in here?"

If Chloe were brave like Elle, she would have lifted the hall pass for them to read and told them that, if they didn't cut class so often, they would be able to read the pass. Nevertheless, she wasn't brave, and they loved inflicting pain as much as Cassandra.

Freezing in place, she tried to tell her legs to get out when they both started coming closer to her, calling her a freak. *Stay still, litt—*

The whoosh from the bathroom door opening had her snapping her head back to see Amo barreling in.

His voice went dark, staring down the two girls who almost had Chloe in their grasp. "What the fuck did you just call her?"

Both girls went pale.

"We're . . . sorry . . . Amo," Stephanie managed to get out.

"I don't want to hear you tell me sorry. You tell Chloe how

fucking sorry you are," he growled at them.

"I-it's okay, Amo. Let's get back to—"

"Now!" he roared over Chloe's voice, ignoring her.

Quickly, the two spat out the words over each other, "I'm sorry."

"I'm sorry, *who?*" he asked.

"I'm sorry, Chloe," they each told her in unison.

"Get the fuck out of here," he spoke coldly.

Never had she seen fear in those girls' faces, but that was all she saw now as they quickly excited the bathroom with their tails between their legs.

Chloe was somewhat envious. She wanted to dart out of there herself. Amo looked and sounded scarier than ever.

When he continued to stand there and stare at her, she wished she had taken her chances with the girls. She had to turn her face so he couldn't see how scared she was.

"W-why aren't you in class?"

"I remembered Stacy and Cassandra bragging about ditching Art." His voice was still dark.

Chloe had to lick her dry lips. "Oh …"

"Hurry up before Mrs. Saylor comes looking for us."

Not until the door slid closed behind him, leaving her alone, did her breath let go.

Amo clenched his fists, wanting to go after those fucking sluts who had been five seconds away from putting their hands all over Chloe. It had taken all the control he had possessed to stay in the bathroom for another minute, knowing if he came out and saw them running down the hallway, he would break their necks in half like he had so desperately wanted to days ago …

"Nero, you didn't tell us we were going to have a party!" The girls bounced up and down the moment Amo and Vincent joined them on Nero's balcony at his house.

Stephanie twirled herself around Amo. "Do we finally get to fuck you?"

He slowly backed her up until her back hit the railing while Vincent was doing the exact thing to Stacy.

As soon as Nero closed the door to the balcony, Amo slid his hand to the back of her head, taking a huge pile of hair in his hands. Suddenly, he jerked down, hearing her neck pop in the process.

Screams, beautiful screams, filled the air …

Wanting to know everyone who had ever laid a hand on Chloe and Elle, they had tricked the two bitches into coming over so they could question them. Not one person was giving out real information about the hell they had put Chloe and Elle through. Stacy and Stephanie had lamely said to ask Chloe, hinting that she had been a part in it, which he didn't believe.

I should have snapped their fucking necks then.

Taking a slow, deep breath, he tried to calm himself. He was trying to change his persona with Chloe, and he had been doing a good job of it until he had walked in on that. After seeing her frightened in there, he could tell he had damage control to do.

Yeah, thanks to those sluts. Let's just hope I can fucking repair it.

Chloe didn't waste time before using the restroom and washing her hands. Amo was leaning against the wall as she came out the door, though she tried her best to avoid eye contact with him.

"Ready?" Amo asked, sounding ... *Chipper?*

She couldn't help looking at him now to see him perfectly fine, like he had been back in the classroom.

She nodded, heading back to class.

"I'm sorry if I scared you. I was just trying to scare them enough so they wouldn't touch you if they ever got you alone again."

She swallowed the lump in her throat. "I-it's okay."

Amo's voice turned sad again. "Everyone just thinks I'm more violent than I actually am."

"You have to be joking." Chloe couldn't help busting out in laughter.

"No." He stopped walking, clearly not liking her laughing at him. "What reason have I given you to think I'm such a mean person?"

Does he have brain damage from all the fights he's been in? An image of him dangling a teenage boy by their neck flashed before her from when Elle and she had caught them at Poison in a fight.

"Um, how about when you were choking that guy Friday?"

"First off, Vincent was the one who started that fight, and I was keeping him from double teaming on Nero. He wasn't trying to play fair, and I didn't want Nero to get hurt."

Chloe blinked at him, trying to process what he had just said.

Crossing her arms, she had another instance come to her. "Okay, then, I saw Sebastian with the black eye as we went home the first day you all sat and ate lunch with us. I'm sure that was you."

"Wow," Amo told her like she had just shot him. "Nero was the one who gave him that black eye, not me."

She didn't want to believe him at first, but he didn't look like he was lying. He actually looked a bit offended.

"You swear you didn't give him the black eye?"

"I swear." Amo put down the hand he had held up.

Chloe was satisfied he was telling the truth then and was able to somewhat relax.

"Nero and Vincent are the mean ones, you know. I'm the nice one."

Glancing at him for a moment, she began to think she might have been too harsh on him. This clearly was a touchy subject for him.

"I guess you will have to prove it." She smiled at him.

He smiled back. "I can do that."

Getting to the door, Amo opened it for her and she rushed inside to hand Mrs. Saylor the hall pass. Sitting back down wasn't as bad as she had expected. Most of the students were focused on their assignments, and Amo's big body blocked their view as they walked down the aisle.

Chloe opened her notebook, settling her nerves so she could start the assignment written on the chalkboard.

Well, I won't tell if you don't. Chloe was going to take this whole thing to her grave. Elle would kill Amo if she ever found out he had gotten her to go to the bathroom. All in all, it wasn't so bad ... She had looked death in the face and survived without Elle having to take a hit for her. Amo might even have a cape underneath that expensive shirt he was wearing.

I'm the nice one.

Gathering her courage, she looked over at him to see him copying her answers. Chloe scooted her chair back to the edge of her table so he couldn't. *Mm-hmm, you're off to a great start of proving it.*

Amo tried not to smile when she took her paper out of view. He honestly couldn't blame her. Mrs. Saylor was a bitch when it came to copying, and he was just trying to come off ... *not as nice.* He obviously wasn't a momma's boy, but out of his friends, he could at least pretend to be the nicest.

Nero was the one who gave him that black eye, not me.

Hey, I wasn't lying. I was just omitting the fact that I had kicked his balls in so hard I made him into the bitch that he is.

THE BACKYARD THAT LOOKED ABSOLUTELY STUNNING

Chloe spent the evening at a dinner party her parents were throwing for some city officials. She had grown used to pretending to listen and smile at these things if she didn't want her father to come to her after it was over. On the inside, though, she was keeping her mind elsewhere, thinking about her encounter with Amo earlier. This time, when she thought of him, no thoughts of the devil came to her, and his dark eyes no longer reminded her of evil black ones.

Elle had been her only friend in years, yet within a week, she felt like she might have gained new ones in Nero, Amo, and Vincent. Yes, it scared her—they scared her—but they were also the best things to happen to Elle and her since their high school year had started. Now all that needed to happen was for Elle to take Nero back.

It was hard for her to believe he had gone out on her, especially after today when he had done nothing but follow them around a few feet back, making sure they were okay. Something was nagging at the back of her mind that it hadn't been what it had looked like. *He's clearly in love with her . . .*

Excusing herself with her father's permission, she went to take a break from it all to get a moment's peace and recharge.

Rinnng.

Chloe answered her cell the moment she saw Elle's name. It was going to help her get a distraction.

"Hey."

A male voice came over, instead. "Hey, Chloe."

"Nero?" Immediately, her nerves were shot. Something wasn't right.

"Elle is fine"—he cleared his throat—"but she was attacked on the way to work. I got her to my house where my doctor is taking care of her. She just suffered a concussion and needs to be monitored through the night."

"I-I—" It was hard for her to even think.

"I promise you she will be okay. I was hoping you would cover for her and tell her parents she is spending the night with yo—"

"I want to see her."

Nero paused. "Okay, I'll send you the address."

Chloe hung up then ran through the house to grab her keys. She slipped out the house, hoping no one would notice her disappearance. It didn't matter to her if they did or if her father would take it out on her; she had to make sure Elle was okay.

When will it all stop? When will Elle quit getting hurt? When will we just be free?

The house looked immaculate as she went up to the door. If it weren't for Elle being there, she wouldn't have been able to do this.

Lightly, she knocked on the door, not expecting the person on the other side.

"W-why are you here?"

Amo practically took up the whole doorframe until he moved out of the way for her to come in. "I came to make sure Elle was okay. Vincent came, too."

Chloe slowly entered, careful to squeeze by Amo. When the door came to a close behind her, her heart stuttered.

"You can wait in the other room for her. She'll be down in a minute."

As she looked around the impressive foyer, the grand, wrought-iron staircase stood out the most.

"I'll wait here." She couldn't help wringing her hands. Worrying about Elle was the only thing she could do on the way over. Not only was she already nervous, but she wanted to be here when she came down.

It's all my fault. The only reason Elle ever got hurt was because of her. If she hadn't needed her as a shield at school, she would be in public school and wouldn't be working in a diner downtown. She'd be... *safe.*

Nodding his head, Amo looked like he was about to head off, but then he stopped.

"I promise you, Chloe, she's going to be fine. We won't let her or you get hurt anymore."

Her heart tugged at that moment as she looked into his eyes. She could tell he meant every word.

"Thank you, Amo."

This time, after he nodded, he left the room and her to her thoughts.

Nero came down the stairs soon after, nodding his head at her just like Amo had done before leaving the room.

Finally, when Elle came down the huge staircase, a little part of her calmed. She looked okay considering what had happened. Then again, Elle was tough and unfortunately used to these things.

Elle quickly noticed her attire of a black, long-sleeved, Peplum dress with black tights and heels. "You didn't leave until it was over, did you?"

Chloe could see the look on Elle's face, showing she was worried that her father was going to make her pay for it. Wanting so badly to lie, she knew there wasn't much of a point because Elle could always tell. Solemnly, she shook her head.

"I'm okay. Thankfully, Nero was there, and that's all that matters." Elle smiled, letting her know she really was all right.

Still unable to find words, she nodded.

Elle decided changing the subject might help. "Do you think Mom will believe I'm spending the night over at your house?"

"I-I don't know."

"What about if I told her we have a project due tomorrow?"

Chloe could feel the tension start to leave her body. "It might work."

"Come in here a second." Nero's loud voice echoed throughout the house.

His yelling certainly broke the tension between them. Looking at each other, they wanted to laugh at the fact that Nero had decided to yell then just to tell them to come here.

Taking a deep breath, she tried to relax. *She's safe now.*

Chloe spent the rest of the evening with Elle at Nero's house. They were introduced to Maria, Nero's sister who was in college. She was surprisingly really nice and drop dead gorgeous. They weren't exactly used to being around a girl who didn't want to kill them, so it took a bit for Chloe to warm up enough to talk to her.

Not knowing whether it was the dinner party from before or the new environment of being at Nero's house, Chloe desperately needed to take a breather. The second she had entered the spacious living room, she had seen a hint of the backyard that looked absolutely stunning. It called to her, made her itch to want to see it for an unknown reason.

"Do you think Nero would mind if I walked out there?" she asked, deciding to take the opportunity of the pizzas arriving for distraction.

"No, he shouldn't." Elle knew that was the only way she would survive any social function. "Go on." She smiled in encouragement.

Chloe walked to the back door and placed her hand on the doorknob. She had been waiting for this all night. Quietly, she slipped out, closing the door behind her. Then, turning around, her breath was taken away by the sight.

There was only one word to describe it: *magical.*

HE WAS NO MAN.
HE WAS THE BOOGIEMAN

PRESENT TIME

The smell of him was what woke her from her long slumber. She hadn't awakened once, still covering herself and clutching Amo's jacket throughout the night. It was the best sleep she had gotten in years, making her wonder if his jacket had ...

She sat up quickly and pulled the material away from her body, placing it on her bed. She found herself staring at it for several minutes, trying to fully remember how she had ended up with it.

The sleepy daze wore off, directing her eyes to her blank white wall, bringing the memory of last night alive ...

Pop. Pop.

The quietest gunshot greeted her ears, trailed by a door squeaking open.

Stay still, little girl ...

Mind going blank, she had no recollection of how she had ended up in the bathtub.

Elle's crying voice seemed so far away as she got in the tub beside her. "Nero, someone's h-here. I think they have a gun."

Or it'll just hurt worse...

The sound of the door breaking in was the last sound she thought she was ever going to hear.

I've come for you ...

Crack.

The sound of broken bones greeted her ears as a baseball bat slammed down onto a limp body.

Snap.

Another flash of the bat making contact with the man's leg, the man who lay practically lifeless on the floor.

He raised the bat once more, pausing only to look her in the eyes. An evil pair of blue-green eyes stared back at her, making her blood run cold. She watched his hands grip the neck of the bat with a force so intense she was positive it was going to shatter before the bat was brought down for its final time.

Crunch.

As she watched the man inhale the air around him, he looked crazed, his appearance disheveled. Then he slicked his overgrown hair back in place, and you could see the slight smile come to his lips.

"Chloe," Amo's voice quietly appeared, trying to bring her back. His jacket was carefully draped over her shoulders after he managed to talk her out of the bathroom.

"Let's get you home."

Coming closer to the evil, blue-green eyes, she gripped the jacket for dear life.

Violence calmed the man before her. He lived off torture, feeding himself by causing pain to others. He had wanted her to see him, see what he was capable of, see who he truly was.

Lucca was his name, but he was no man.

He was the boogieman.

She had only witnessed that in one other being in her life: the devil.

WHEN I LEAVE

After that day, it brought back too many memories, and she then found herself in the same haunting place after she had been kidnapped in freshman year. Since then, she only ever hung out with Elle and Amo. And throughout the summer, she had found herself decreasing the amount she spent with them… More… And more…

It's going to make it easier on them… for when I leave.

WHEN YOU'RE SITTING IN CALIFORNIA. AND I'M MISSING YOU

"**C**hloe, please! Just one dance!*" Elle yelled at her over the blasting music.

Chloe violently shook her head as she sat uncomfortably at the high top table with the loud-ass music in her ears. She wondered how in the world she had let Elle talk her into coming to Poison on her birthday.

"You promised me you would go out for your birthday!"

Oh, yeah, I did. She guilt me into it.

Vincent's girlfriend, Lake—*yes, the world is still on its axis*—screamed over the music. "Come on, Chloe, you ditched us practically all summer!"

That wasn't completely true; she just didn't hang out with them all at once anymore, especially at Nero and Vincent's new apartments downtown. The last time she had hung out with them there, a gunman had almost killed them.

"Go dance. I'll be fine!" Chloe yelled at them. This place wasn't for a girl like her.

She watched her friends roll their eyes before they grabbed their boyfriends up and took them to the dancefloor.

Watching Elle with Nero, she finally found a sort of peace within a part of her. She had hated herself so much for so long over how she had treated Elle. Chloe would never forgive herself for it, but the one thing she had done right was that she had always rooted for Nero. After all these years of Elle being a hero, it was time she found someone to be her armor.

Elle never needed a hero. Elle would never quit being one, either. But what she did need was help. Every great hero needed some type of shield to protect them. Nero was her perfect match, and that was one thing Chloe had seen from day one.

She's going to be happier without me.

Whereas Elle was the hero saving her day in and day out, Chloe was the weak, little victim who only brought pain to her. Chloe was still broken beyond repair, and as long as she stayed here, Elle would continue to try to fix her.

For once in her life, she needed to be the hero for Elle so she could live a life free of Chloe. And for once, she needed to be the hero for herself and leave her family and this city behind with all its bad memories so she could find peace.

Amo came up behind her, setting a bottle of water down in front of her. "You'll regret it, you know."

"Regret what?" She smiled at him, pretending to be happy.

Amo scooted in as close to her as he could without touching her so she could hear him. "When you're sitting in California, missing Elle, you'll regret that you didn't go dance with her once."

Looking back at her best friend, she saw that Elle looked so free.

"She looks happy right now. I'll always remember watching her dance, and that's good enough for me."

The next song was louder than the last, making Amo lean down to whisper in her ear. "Will you dance with me, then?"

His breath was warm as it touched her skin, his body just a few inches away. It was the closest he had ever been to her, making the hairs stand up on the back of her neck.

"When you're sitting in California, and I'm missing you, I'll regret that I didn't get to dance with you once."

Chloe looked over into his dark eyes that carried a hidden sparkle and felt a tug at her heart. Amo had managed to crawl his way into a place in her heart in such a short amount of time of being friends. He never failed to make her laugh; he always tried to make her as comfortable as possible; and the best part about him was he never forced her to tell him anything. He accepted her for who she was and didn't want her to meet her demons, always making sure she was as happy as she could be with him.

Amo moved just an inch closer. "Please ... for me?"

She didn't know how to say no to him in that moment, didn't know how she could possibly turn down something that looked so meaningful to him. *I'll regret it, too.*

Before she could change her mind, she nodded. The look that crossed his face would be what she always remembered every time she thought of him.

Standing up, Amo led the way. Thankfully, it was almost closing time, so everyone was mostly gone, and the dancefloor had plenty of space for her.

"Yay!" Elle yelled when she nervously joined them on the dancefloor.

Saying she was nervous was an understatement as she awkwardly tried to dance with them. When she looked ready to walk off, Amo's pleading eyes were the only things that kept her in place.

Come on, this is one of the last times you get to have fun with them. She pepped talked herself into trying again and made herself try to let go for one night. Finally, when they all started dancing silly like you would see at a wedding, she relaxed enough to get into it.

It was honestly the most fun she had ever had, enjoying every second of them collectively singing horribly and dancing ridiculously.

"This is the last song of the night!" the DJ came over the microphone after a song ended.

"Boo!" They all called out, not wanting it to end.

As they danced to the last song, Nero pulled Elle in closer while Vincent pulled Lake in closer for a final dance. Chloe was tired and about to walk off to go retrieve her water, but Amo stopped her.

"It's the last one, and I want my own dance to remember when you're at Stanford." He came in closer to her.

I really wish he would quit saying that. She couldn't say no to him whenever he did that.

The adrenaline from dancing was still pumping through her, so she stayed to finish the final dance. Trying her best to dance one on one with him was hard, though, considering they weren't touching each other.

Amo got in closer to her, putting very little space between them, turning the dance serious. Chloe's heart pumped so hard she thought it was going to come out of her chest. Somehow, though, she managed to sway her hips to the beat.

Staring up at him, she saw something different come alive in him. It looked like Amo was going to come in closer … But then the music stopped.

"I knew you could do it. Wasn't that so much fun, Chloe!" Elle interrupted whatever was happening between them, and it wasn't hard to miss the unhappy reaction from Amo.

Heart still pumping, she looked over to Elle, hopefully managing some sort of a smile. "Yeah, that was fun."

Leaving the lounge, Chloe said her good-byes to Elle, Nero, Lake, and Vincent as they wished her a final happy birthday.

"I'll walk you to your car," Amo told her when she went to say good-bye to him.

"Okay." Her voice sounded breathy from all the dancing.

Walking to her car together, she could feel the tension build again between them until she reached her car.

"Thank you for dancing with me." He looked down at her, grinning. "You're not so bad."

Chloe couldn't help laughing. "Oh, thanks. You weren't as terrible as I thought you would be, either."

He laughed back. "Well, I had fun, and when you leave me to go to Stanford—"

"I am not leaving you. Don't say it like that!"

Amo stepped in closer to her. "So you're not leaving, then?"

"Well ..." She thought about her words carefully. "Yes, but it's not like I want to."

"Then don't."

"You know I have to, Amo ..." *He makes it sound so easy.* "What I meant was that I don't want to leave Elle ..." Her voice trailed off to find the courage for her next words. "Or you."

His tall frame leaned down to meet her short one. "Are you going to miss me?"

With his face so close to hers, she felt her heart begin to pound again. It took her a minute to find the words, and when she did, they came out breathy again. "Of course."

All she could hear was the pounding of her heart getting louder and louder in her ears.

Unable to pull her eyes away, she realized what she had seen in them on the dancefloor: hunger.

Amo's face came slowly closer to hers, and the pounding only grew louder, faster as she held her breath. His lips were so close to hers, yet right before they came crashing down, Chloe found her breath and turned her face away.

Seeing her face now covered by her hair and breathing heavily, he took a deep breath. "I'm sorry, Chloe."

As she desperately tried to get her breath and nerves under control from almost being kissed, she kept her eyes on the ground. Then she opened her car door to escape the closeness between them.

He watched her get in and grabbed the door before she could close it. "I shouldn't have tried that without asking. Please forgive me."

Taking a deep breath, she hoped to find the words.

"I-it's okay." She just needed to get away for space. After being surrounded by so many people all night, it felt like it was hitting her all at once. "I-I promise."

Amo stared at her for a moment then swiftly nodded his head. "Happy Birthday, Chloe," he told her right before shutting the door.

Watching him walk away, she dug her nails deep into her palms. She thought she had been doing so good tonight, almost like she wasn't plagued by human contact.

I thought for once I might be normal . . .

Drawing first blood only made her dig deeper.

I thought for once I wasn't a freak.

Fuck! Fuck! FUCK!

Amo could hear the clock ticking. Time was almost up. He had been so careful to go slowly with her, working day in and day out to get her used to him. Now that his time was almost up, he had been getting ballsy, trying anything to get close to her. However, he was afraid he might have gone too far.

He couldn't help it. The second he had seen her in that black dress that clung to her curvy figure, he had wanted his hands all over her body and his lips all over her beautiful face. Every day he spent with her, he just fell deeper and deeper, finding something different to admire about her.

To him, she was perfect, inside and out.

All he wanted was for Chloe to stay and continue their friendship. If he could get her to do that, then he could be patient and take as long as she needed for them to become more.

I would wait forever for her if that's what it took.

THAT WAY, HE KNOWS I'M REALLY GONE . . . AND I'M NOT COMING BACK

"*Have you finished packing?*"

Chloe zipped the large suitcase closed, struggling to slide it from the bed. "Almost. I have so many clothes, they won't fit." She stared at the two suitcases that were already filled, the zippers threatening to break. "Do you have a suitcase I can—"

"I need the ones I have. Besides, they won't match," her mother snapped.

Her suitcases are black. How wouldn't they match? Her mother knew she wouldn't ever see any of her suitcases again if she lent one to her. Just like Chloe had no plans to see her once she boarded the plane to California.

"That's okay. I'll run out tomorrow and buy one." Chloe sank onto the edge of her bed as her mother walked around, surveying the sterile room that had been her bedroom since her father had moved her into this house after becoming mayor.

"You're going to take that broken music box?" she asked resentfully, looking at it sitting on her nightstand waiting to be packed.

The music box that no longer played had been her late aunt's, the one who died while giving birth to her. She had taken one look at it and fallen in love. She could still remember opening the present her father gave to her, turning the key, and listening to the tune over and over again until her mother had made her stop.

"I'm going to pack it in my backpack with my laptop as a carry-on. I won't have to worry about it getting more damaged."

"Well ... I'll go. You don't need my help. Good night."

Chloe sat on the bed, watching the door close and wanting her ghost tears to be real. Neither of her parents were going to miss her. She could see them going out to eat in an expensive restaurant and toasting to each other that she would be gone when they returned home.

Ring.

Chloe picked up her phone from her nightstand, and Elle's voice came over the phone.

"Are you still awake?"

"Yes. What are you still doing awake?"

"Nero decided he wanted pizza. I have to go get my parking permit for college the day your flight leaves. What time is your flight?"

"Eleven a.m."

Elle let out a breath. "That's good. I can pick up my permit after one."

"I told you, you shouldn't come. We will just stand around, crying." She'd had this conversation with her so many times. It was going to be too hard on both of them if she came. When the tears didn't fall down her face, it was going to break Elle's heart.

"How about we do something tomorrow? You know I'm going to see you before you leave, Chloe."

She shook her head. "But I have to finish packing and go to the mall to get a few last minute things and buy another suitcase—"

"Okay, then I will meet you at the mall tomorrow." Elle's voice held a smile.

Dang it . . . Even if she protested, Elle was going to be there.

"You're not going to make it easy for me to leave, are you?"

"Nope!" Elle said, her smile more prominent through the phone. "Listen, you know Nero and Amo want to come to say one last good-bye, too."

Chloe had somehow expected her to say that. She wasn't sure if she could face Amo again, not after last night. The almost kiss had been a disappointment for Amo, but to her, it had been the only way she could live with herself. Staying in Kansas City wasn't an option. She had watched Elle protect her through high school, and she wouldn't watch another friend get hurt because of her.

Say good-bye to him.

It was going to be her last chance, and this way, everyone would be there. It wouldn't be so awkward.

Chloe huffed loudly through the phone. "Who are you going to boss when I'm gone?"

A mischievous laughter came through the phone. "I plan to harass you by text message. See you tomorrow!"

Chloe lay down on her bed when the call ended. The thought of seeing Amo again was making her nervous. However, she wanted to say good-bye to him officially.

That way, he knows I'm really gone … And I'm not coming back.

A CHOICE MUST BE MADE

Chloe and Elle sat in the food court, watching Nero and Amo get food. She had insisted on getting her own food, but Amo wasn't having it. The tension between them was still uncomfortable, but it wasn't nearly as bad as if they had been alone.

"I can't believe you're actually going to leave." Elle looked like she was about to get emotional. "I mean, I knew you would; I just thought you might change your mind."

"You know I don't want to leave you, but you know I can't stay here, either."

"I know. I just always thought we would be going to college together," Elle whispered.

Chloe had, too. They hadn't expected Elle to fall in love.

"If I hate it after a semester, I can always come back and go to the university here with you, and we can spend summers together."

Elle started tearing up. "I'm just going to miss you so much."

"Please don't cry." Chloe's heart started to break. This was why she definitely couldn't handle Elle going to the airport with her. "You will always be my best friend. I wouldn't be here if it weren't for you, and I thank you for protecting me when I couldn't. I love you, Elle." She might not be able to hug her and show her love, but she could at least tell her.

"I love you, too, Chloe." A tear dripped down her face.

Chloe smiled at her as they enjoyed this moment together. "Okay, now stop with the crying. You're going to ruin your makeup."

Elle laughed as she wiped away the tear.

"I hope I'm not interrupting," a sweet voice butted in.

Turning, Chloe saw Nero's sister Maria.

"Elle told me you were leaving, and I wanted to see you before you left. I hope you don't mind. Plus, it was a good excuse to come shopping," Maria joked, taking a seat beside Elle.

Chloe's eyes traveled to the man behind her, and she held her breath when his blue-green eyes settled on her. She hadn't seen him since he had gripped that bat in his hands. Truthfully, she hadn't seen Maria since then, either.

Chloe, Elle, and Lake had been in Nero's apartment when a gunman had broken into the apartment, expecting Maria to be there. However, she had been sick and hadn't come. Chloe never liked to ask questions about why someone had tried to go after Maria, because she didn't feel it was her business.

Maria was everything a girl ever wanted to be. She was tall, blonde, and looked like a supermodel. Chloe was convinced she was, considering she always came with bodyguards. Even though she enjoyed Maria's company, she didn't ever feel comfortable with her. After all, not only had she almost died the last time she had tried to spend time with her, but most of the time, Maria's bodyguard ended up being Lucca.

She barely managed to pull her eyes back to Maria. "I-I don't mind." She twisted her hands under the table. "Thank you for coming."

Chloe's eyes moved back to the man who was now coming closer to the table. His dark appearance didn't remind her so much of their last encounter. Instead, it reminded her of their meetings under the white gazebo in the Caruso's backyard. The first time she had met him was the night Elle had been attacked while going to work. Elle had been terrified of him at the time, but she had also found him attractive. Any attractiveness she had seen in him had disappeared the night he had crashed a bat down ruthlessly, showing her his true self. Or so she had thought ...

She had expected to be horrified and disgusted if she ever saw him again; instead, she found just found him ... chilling.

Lucca's cold voice shivered up her spine. "Still running away, darlin'?"

She slowly nodded her head, knowing exactly what he meant by running. He seemed to somehow always know the hidden secrets she kept locked away.

Amo came to the table then, setting down a tray of food in front of Chloe. He seemed to stare Lucca down for a moment before he took a seat beside her.

Lucca kept his eyes on Amo for an extra second before he turned his gaze back to Chloe. "Be careful out there, darlin'; you won't have anyone to save you if you get into trouble."

Watching him leave to take a seat at the table behind Maria, she saw he sat down, facing her. It felt like he was looking into her soul.

"Chloe, are you going to eat?" Amo's voice finally had her looking away.

"Y-yeah." Trying to shake off Lucca staring at her, she did her best to ignore him as she picked up some fries.

"Are you all packed up, Chloe?" Maria asked, stealing some of Nero and Elle's fries that he had brought to the table.

She could see another scary man take a seat beside Lucca. *Another bodyguard?* She swallowed hard. Another bodyguard meant it was bad for Maria.

"For the most part."

Lucca's eyes had yet to move from her. You could always feel his eyes on you. It was like his gaze created ice on your skin.

"What time does your flight leave?" Amo asked as he slung his arm over the back of her chair.

She didn't know why she looked at Lucca when he did that, but she could feel him wanting to slowly kill Amo. She had seen that look on him before when he had taken a baseball bat to a lifeless body.

"E-eleven."

Amo leaned in closer to her, almost brushing her shoulder when he stole a fry off her plate. "In the morning?"

She could imagine it now, imagine Lucca killing Amo. It was like the fury in his death glare was painting a picture in her mind.

Somehow, she managed a nod. Between Amo's close body and Lucca's daggers being thrown from his eyes, she didn't know what was going on. She wanted to rip her skin off; she was that uncomfortable.

I can't take it! Quickly, she stood from the table, grabbing her purse. "I'm not hungry. I'm going to get my suitcase."

"I can go wi—"

"No. Stay," she cut Amo off then took a quick, calming breath. "I-it's just right there. I'll be back in a minute." She quickly walked away, leaving stunned faces behind.

She headed to the luggage store that was right at the beginning of the food court.

Calm down, Chloe, she told herself, reaching the safety of the store that was far enough away from Amo and Lucca to breathe.

Staring at the suitcases, she managed to ignore what had just happened enough to pick the size she needed then wheeled it to the checkout counter. The line was so long it curved the registers. Waiting for her turn, she patiently stood. However, the longer she waited in line, the stronger a feeling came over her that she was being watched.

Looking around, she didn't see them at the tables anymore. When she scanned the food court, she found Elle, Nero, and Amo waiting in line to get a pretzel. They loved the pizza pretzels and always had to get one to take home for later. She noticed Amo glance in her direction, but he wasn't the one she felt staring at her.

Scanning the other side of the food court, she then saw Maria in a small shoe store with her bodyguard. However, Lucca stood by the shoe store door, watching the passerby's until his eyes settled on her. Still, his stare wasn't what brought the feeling that was taking over her body.

With it only getting stronger, she was about to get out of line, when a woman's voice stopped her. "Will that be all?"

Nodding her head, she handed the sales clerk the suitcase to ring it up then her credit card, wanting to quickly leave. While the cashier charged her card, she looked out the window into the mall and met the eyes her nightmares were made of. Clutching the counter, she kept telling herself frantically she was imagining the face staring back at her.

"Here you go. Thank you. Come again."

Chloe snapped her eyes back to the woman behind the counter then back to the spot she had seen ... *He's not there.*

Letting out her breath and trying to control her racing heart, she realized it had just been another figment of her imagination. *Lucca is doing this to you.*

"T-thanks." She took her card and suitcase.

Many times, the devil haunted her sleep or even when she was awake. This time, it felt more real than usual. Only one other time had it felt so real, and Lucca had been there. *See? It's just him.*

Coming out of the store, she rolled her suitcase behind her as she scanned the mall. She found Amo, Nero, and Elle checking out on one side of the food court, and on the other side, Lucca still guarded the shoe store with Maria.

Taking a step forward, she found herself freezing in place, a horrible feeling rocking through her body.

Stay still, little girl.

Bang. Bang.

Chaos ensued as gunshots rang throughout the air behind her. Screaming people ran as fast as their legs could take them to the exit at the back of the food court.

Nero protected Elle, running toward the exit, while Maria's bodyguard protected her, also heading toward the exit.

Unable to find her legs, she felt like everything was going in slow motion as people ran past her.

Or it'll just hurt worse.

"Chloe!" Amo's voice boomed as he tried to move forward to get to her, but the running people were coming at him, making it impossible.

Her heart thudded once in her ear as she took a step toward Amo.

"Chloe, *move*," Lucca demanded from the other side, fighting against the flood of people, trying to reach her.

Her heart thudded again, and she took another step forward, this time toward Lucca.

"*This* way, Chloe," Amo pleaded.

"*To me*, Chloe!" Lucca demanded.

Time stood still before her as she looked at the two men desperately trying to fight their way to her. They both stood equal distances apart from her. Her mind felt pulled to the right toward Amo, yet her body felt pulled to the left toward Lucca.

As she looked at Amo, memories flashed before her ...

Smiling proudly, he took his seat. "You thought I wasn't going to actually sit beside you, didn't you?"

Chloe's answer was scooting her chair over to the very edge, though it didn't give her much more room because he practically took up the whole table.

By his smirk disappearing, she could tell he didn't like her answer very much ...

... When a tray was extended to her, she looked up to see Amo holding it out for her. It was the first time she could see something that almost seemed nice under his rough exterior.

Slowly, she took it from him, having to look away as she did. She had grown almost used to the roughness of him, and seeing him differently for once seemed weird ...

... "You know why they're staring like that, don't you?"

She looked to the floor. "Because they think I'm a fre—"

"No, you're not a freak," Amo snapped. He paused for just an instant before he said, "It's because they've never seen me walk a girl to class before." ...

... "Place your hands on the table," he whispered over to her.

She quickly shook her head and started to press her nails into the skin.

"Please, Chloe, I can't take you doing that to yourself," he pleaded.

When she glanced at him, it was the first time she really looked at him, like really *looked into his eyes. They weren't the black abyss staring back at her like she had always thought. They might have been dark, but they also had a lightness to them. Almost like a sparkle of silver running through giving them life. They were dark yet light, reminding her of yin and yang.*

Taking a breath, she placed her hands on the table . . .

. . . The next song was louder than the last, making Amo lean down to whisper in her ear. "Will you dance with me, then?"

His breath was warm as it touched her skin, his body just a few inches away. It was the closest he had ever been to her, making the hairs stand up on the back of her neck.

"When you're sitting in California, and I'm missing you, I'll regret that I didn't get to dance with you once."

She now turned her eyes to Lucca, the memory of when they first met flashing . . .

"Hey, darlin'," a deep voice sounded behind her.

Chloe jumped at the sound. A second later, a man appeared on the other side of the rails. He was terrifyingly beautiful and scared the hell out of her, regardless of how handsome he was. She didn't think a man that good-looking should even exist, or a man that chilling.

Chloe didn't move a muscle, completely frozen in place.

He kept walking toward the entrance of the gazebo and went up the step. "I didn't mean to scare you."

She had no idea how she hadn't heard him. She didn't even know where he had come from.

She watched him lean up on a pillar, blocking her exit. After every hair had managed to stand up on her body at one look of his eyes, Chloe darted her gaze down to her lap and started fiddling with her hands.

"I'm Nero's brother, Lucca. I would shake your hand, but you wouldn't shake it, anyway."

Chloe quickly glanced back up at him before looking down again. How did he know that?

Lucca read her eyes. "I overheard that you're apparently germaphobic."

Chloe glanced back up at him again. Apparently? He was really starting to freak her out now.

Chloe attempted to decide if she should honestly be afraid and try to run away. Yes, I should. However, Lucca was blocking the only exit, and she was not going anywhere near him.

Chloe saw him move; as a result, she regretfully had to look at him again. She held her breath when he put his hand into his pocket to pull something out. When a pack of cigarettes came out, she let out her breath. She continued to watch him pull a cigarette out and then hold it between his lips as he put the pack back in his pocket. Going into his other pocket, he pulled out a lighter. Chloe thought she was going to have a heart attack if he went into his pocket again.

Lucca flipped his lighter open and lit the end, making it burn a bright red as he inhaled.

"You don't mind, do you?"

Chloe slowly shook her head. She wished she could look away from him, but she was too afraid. She could tell he was Nero's brother without a doubt; they both oozed confidence and sex. They looked very similar, as well.

Lucca had the same skin color, but she couldn't quite tell if his hair was black or brown. The same went with his eyes; she couldn't tell if they were blue or green. She would swear they were one color before the string lights picked up the other color, changing her mind all over again. Lucca, however, was a billion times more *frightening and a million times more handsome than Nero. She figured it had to do with the age gap, but one thing they were very different about was the way they dressed. Nero only dressed in button-up shirts and slacks, while Lucca was wearing a black sweatshirt and dark, loose jeans.*

She wasn't used to seeing hair as long as his. It was swept back, yet it touched the back of his neck. He clearly didn't care if it wasn't trimmed and neat, just like his unshaven stubble. Everyone she was around always looked immaculate, making his bad-boy appearance more like 'don't cross me, or I will murder your entire family tree.' I don't think it matters what he wears; he would look like that, regardless.

"Aren't you a little cold out here, darlin'?" His voice also oozed just as much confidence as Nero.

She felt uncomfortable with him calling her that. If I tell him my name, he'll stop.

"M-my name is Chloe."

She watched him smile as he took a puff, holding the cigarette between his thumb and index finger. He exhaled. "The mayor's daughter, right?"

Chloe nodded gently. She knew that practically everyone was aware she was the mayor's only child. Right?

"You were in that car wreck a few years back. I remember reading about it in the papers. Is that how you tell everyone you got those scars?" Lucca tapped his ashes in the snow without moving his eyes from her.

Chloe swallowed and looked back down at her hands. "That i-is how I got them."

"No, it's not. I know a knife cut when I see one."

Chloe glimpsed back up at him. How did he know? *"I-I d-don't know what you're t-talking about."*

Lucca flicked his cigarette in the yard. "Yeah, you do."

A chill went down her spine at his words, causing her to stand, not able to stay around him any longer and not liking where this was headed.

She walked a step forward, hoping he would move. His muscular frame was blocking the whole entryway. She didn't want to know how many hours he'd spent in the gym; she could see his muscles through his thick, dark sweatshirt. When he still didn't move, she gradually moved up more. Please move, please move.

Chloe was now just a few small steps away, refusing to go any farther. "C-can you let me through?" Her legs started to shake when he dipped his hand back into his pocket. Her heels made it hard for her to hold herself up.

Lucca pulled out another cigarette and flipped his lighter open. He slowly lit the end, not moving his eyes from her. He blew the smoke out, making it roll over her body. Instead of putting the lighter back in his pocket, he flicked it again, and the silver Zippo shot out a flame. Lucca did one of his tricks, rolling the lighted Zippo in-between each of his fingers.

"I will if you tell me how old you are."

Wait ... what?

Chloe became entranced, staring at the flame expertly passing through his fingers. She didn't know how he didn't let it burn himself.

Chloe mindlessly answered and asked her own question, captivated by the glow. "Seventeen. You?"

Lucca suddenly flipped the lighter closed. "Twenty-six."

Something told her he wasn't very happy about her answer by the look on his face.

Twenty-six. She had no clue why she'd asked how old he was.

After she'd watched him move slightly to let her pass, she really wished he would give her more room than that.

Chloe slowly walked up and turned her body to the side, keeping her eyes on *him, afraid he would move when she passed through. She held her breath as she carefully started to move by him. Her face came to the middle of his chest, even in heels, and his shoulders came right above her head.*

When she had successfully passed him, somehow with just mere centimeters apart, Chloe started walking as fast as she could, trying not to run back to the house.

Lucca's voice carried across the yard. "You can't run from the truth forever, darlin'."

Chloe picked her feet up faster.

Yes, I can. I've been doing it for years . . .

She picked up her feet, going toward the man with the blue-green eyes who commanded her body . . .

Crack.

The sound of broken bones greeted her ears as a baseball bat slammed down into a limp body.

Snap.

Another flash of the bat making contact with the man's leg, the man who lay practically lifeless on the floor.

He raised the bat once more, pausing only to look her in the eyes. An evil pair of blue-green eyes stared back at her, making her blood run cold. She watched him grip the neck of the bat with a force so intense she was positive it was going to shatter before the bat was brought down for its final time.

Crunch.

As she watched the man inhale the air around him, he looked crazed, his appearance disheveled. Then he slicked his overgrown hair back in place, and you could see the slight smile come to his lips.

Turning her eyes back to Amo, she saw him screaming, horror gripping his face to get to her, to save her . . .

"I'm the nice one."

Glancing at him for a moment, she began to think she might have been too harsh on him. This clearly was a touchy subject for him.

"I guess you will have to prove it." She smiled at him.

He smiled back. "I can do that. . ."

There was always a moment in time one faced in life when a choice must be made, and this was her moment.

Time unfroze. She kicked her feet up off the ground, running into the arms of the man she had chosen to protect her. His arms circled around her as she took a shuddering breath. They were the first arms to hold her in years.

Holding her close, Amo whispered into her ear, "I've got you."

I CAN'T BE FIXED. NOT BY YOU, NOT BY ANYONE. I'M JUST BROKEN

hloe squeezed her hands together on her lap, silently staring ahead as Amo drove her home.

Lucca's face was going to haunt her for the rest of her life. The look he had given her as Amo carried her out of the mall was one she would never forget. It wasn't going to haunt her because it scared her; it was going to haunt her because the look in his eyes had shattered her. He didn't even meet her eyes when he ordered Amo to immediately take her home.

"Is the air conditioning too cold?"

Lucca's face disappeared from her mind at Amo's question.

"N-no."

What had her shivering was not only Lucca's face, but also

sitting in the car with Amo. His dark gaze kept coming to her face as if he wanted to say something.

She was so tense it was a relief when he finally pulled into her driveway. Chloe brought her hand to the door handle, prepared to jump out of the car.

"Wait." She froze at his word. "Stay and go to college here … with Elle and Lake." Amo shifted in his seat to face her fully. "I could take some classes. Who is going to walk you to class when Elle or I aren't there?"

Chloe kept her gaze down, looking at him through her lashes. "I'll have to get used to being on my own."

"But if you stayed here, you wouldn't have to."

What had happened at the mall hadn't changed anything for her. It had only solidified that she had to keep running.

"Elle won't have to watch out for me anymore. She can finally enjoy school at college with me not getting in her way. I want that for her."

"What about you? What about me?" He tried to keep his voice even.

"I'll adjust. It will be good for me. You have Nero and Vincent and your job at the casino hotel to keep you so busy you won't even remember me."

"I'll remember you …" Amo whispered.

Her heart started to hurt for him. She could feel her resolve begin to slip away. If she didn't get out of this car, she was afraid he might change her mind.

"That you walked me to class for a few months? That my best friend is your friend's girlfriend?"

Amo pounded his hand on the steering wheel. "You're not like any other girl I know, Chloe." Calming his breathing, he whispered the words, "I love you."

Chloe's heart beat against her chest. That was exactly what she had been afraid of.

Jumping out of the car, she ran toward her front door. *He can't. He can't love me.*

"Fucking wait!" Amo ran to her with pleading eyes.

Kill it. You have to kill what's between us so you won't kill him . . .

"We're friends, Amo. If I stay . . . I can't. I will never be what you want. You need a girl like Elle or Lake. Even a girl like Cassandra would be better than me. You love being with your friends, and I like being alone. That's why I'm leaving," she lied for Amo's sake. He deserved a normal girl, not someone who was afraid of her own shadow.

"No one likes to be alone," he told her softly.

Chloe wished she could brush away normal tears, not the ghost tears that wanted to fall down her cheeks.

"I'm not normal; I'm a freak." Taking a harsh breath, she hated herself for the words she was about to say. "You said so yourself."

Amo paled.

"Fucking freak!" was said, followed by laughter filling the space with continuous echoes of the word "freak."

She had watched him mouth the word freshman year as she entered the lunchroom for the first time with her new scars.

He looked away from her. "Why didn't you say something?"

"What was I suppose say?" Chloe put her hands on the front door. "Bye, Amo."

Tears filled his eyes. "I didn't mean it . . ."

I know you didn't.

"It's okay, Amo. We're even. I called you a beast." She opened the door, going inside. Then she reached out to close the door. "I can't be fixed. Not by you, not by anyone. I'm just broken." Shutting the door and closing out his glossy dark gaze somehow broke her even more than she already was.

Chloe wiped the scar on her cheek, feeling moisture. A single real tear had finally fallen.

I'm so sorry, Amo . . .

Chloe quickly shoved her suitcases into the trunk of her car, wanting to be long gone before her parents got back from a dinner after his City Council meeting. The last suitcase, which she had actually taken from her mom's closet since she hadn't been able to retrieve the one she had bought, was finally shoved in.

After Amo had left, Chloe had decided she needed to leave . . . *now.* She was afraid to see how she felt in the morning, and she didn't want to give Amo a chance to meet her at the airport before her flight took off. Therefore, she had called and gotten her flight changed to leave in three hours.

She had written two notes. One was for Lana, which she had left in the cleaning closet, telling her that she loved her and not to worry about her and also how she was sorry she didn't say good-bye to her face. The second note was for her parents, telling them that she had decided to leave early and that the key to her car would be placed in the hidden key box above her tire.

It was sad that the one she had said I love you to wasn't the one you would think.

Getting in the car, Chloe took one last look at the house that had never been a home, but had been her prison. As she drove away, she could feel the chains slowly start to break as she left her prison and then her city behind. Breaking free was a paramount feeling she would always remember.

Chloe rolled down the window, letting the warm summer air whip across her face. Taking a deep breath in, she felt the last chain break.

I've finally reached freedom.

It was going to be close, but she would make the plane. Most of her time was spent trying to find the correct parking area.

Chloe parked her car in the desolate-looking parking garage. Pulling out her suitcases and backpacks, she locked her doors then went to her rear wheel. Her fingers fumbled as they searched for the hidden key box that was stuck to the underside of the car.

Bending down farther to look for it, her fingers finally grasped the box.

"Got i—"

A hard body wrapped around her, along with a cloth covering

her mouth and nose. The hand behind the cloth stifled any screams or protests she could have made, and the strong body kept her in place.

Stay still, little girl.

There was no fight to be had. Her vision went blurry as it all started to fade away.

Or it'll just hurt worse.

She had known it was too good to be true. Her soul belonged to the devil …

THE STORY BEHIND THE SCAR. THE STORY OF SADNESS. GRIEF. AND TORTURE

SEVEN MONTHS EARLIER

Pulling his classic black Cadillac onto the side of the street, he positioned himself perfectly to watch the house. Then he looked at the clock and saw he had timed it perfectly. *School's out.*

He flipped his lighter off and on, off and on, waiting for her return. Lucca had never been good at sitting still, nor was he a very patient man when he was tired. The night before had been a long one, and his body still felt it this afternoon. Regardless, he had enjoyed every second of it.

Last night, he had lain Mr. Johnson to rest and held up his promise of fucking the blonde until she regretted it. Both things had satiated his dark side . . . *for now, anyway.*

Lucca flipped his lighter closed as a stuck-up BMW pulled into the driveway. He had never trusted a German car. The only thing good about it was its black paint color.

A strawberry blonde exited the car. *Elle Buchanan.* He couldn't help the sneer he pasted on his face. His little brother was in big fucking trouble.

Watching her walk to the front door, he believed the girl only got prettier the more you looked at her.

It's going to be a shame when I have to strangle the life out of her.

One thing was for sure, the girl was going to die, and nothing was going to save her. It was unfortunate she had been there when the trigger had been pulled, but some girls were just born unlucky, this one in particular. She was only going to make it another month to her eighteenth birthday.

The stuck-up looking car reversed, drawing back his attention. He wondered who would drop off a girl in this neighborhood. Truthfully, he was a little shocked this was the address, considering the girl had come from a prep school.

Looking at the clock again, he noticed there was a bit of time before Elle went to work. His gut told him to follow the car. Anyone she hung out with could possibly be collateral damage if her fucking mouth blabbed too much.

Lucca started his car, deciding to follow the BMW. He kept a good distance back, following it in a direction he hadn't been expecting. This part of town was mostly owned by the city, along with some expensive restaurants and shops.

Watching the car pull into one of the most expensive shops in town, he parked on the street and pulled out his cell phone to text the license plate number to a friend. He waited in anticipation, the curiosity slowly eating away at him, only growing worse when the car door opened.

Immediately, he knew it was a woman when tall, black boots and black jeans hit the ground. The next thing he noticed was her long, silky hair. It was the blackest hair he had ever seen.

He desperately wanted a glimpse of her face, but she never turned around.

Lucca found himself turning off the car and getting out, wondering how this was more important than anything else he could do with his time. His instincts were what kept him going, following her into the store.

Lucca prided himself on being able to go unnoticed. His appearance of dark jeans, black shirts, and black sweatshirts allowed him to do that, plus his scruffy face and hair. He could go places no one in the family could go. Made men demanded attention with their suits and immaculate grooming, whereas he didn't need that kind of attention. *I have other ways to get the attention I demand.*

Entering the store undetected was easy with all the expensive shit it held. He navigated the store, finding the girl in all black who seemed to be looking for a particular piece. A slight glimpse of the left side of her face revealed her soft porcelain skin. He stalked closer.

Have I seen her before?

Another small glimpse revealed her young age.

Stopping, he was about to turn around. *She's too young.*

The girl turned then went back to a table she had missed.

His heart stopped a beat when he saw the whole left side of her face and a striking gray eye. The other half of her face was covered by a veil of hair. He wished he could reach out to feel the pure black strands of silk and move it to reveal the rest of her face.

Leave now. Nothing good would come of this. He should have left the moment he had noticed she was just a teenage girl.

He was unable to place it yet, but something about her called to him. It kept him from looking away from the girl and leaving.

The whole thing felt so wrong yet so right. He was being pulled in different directions. His mind told him to leave, but his body kept him patiently waiting.

Watching her hand go up to her face, he felt his breath catch in his throat when she swept her hair behind her ear. *Fuck.*

His heart skipped another beat at the sight of her face in its entirety. His eyes traveled down the right side of her gorgeous face that held a scar from above her eyebrow down to the hollow of her cheek. Another one graced the right side above and below her luscious lips. The instinct to let his fingertips glide down each mark was so strong he thought he might break his cover.

Her gray eyes held the story behind the scar, a story of sadness, grief, and torture. It was like staring at a perfect porcelain doll that had been dropped one too many times. Others would see a flaw in the cracked doll, making her no longer perfect, but he saw only beauty. She was the most beautiful creature he had ever seen.

He could watch her study the delicate piece with gentle hands for hours.

The gold, ornate piece she was infatuated with was unfamiliar to him until she opened the egg-shaped object, and music began to play. Her eyes danced as she watched a ballerina twirl to the music. He wondered what it would feel like if she looked at him that way.

"It's a beautiful piece, isn't it?" the older woman who looked to be the storeowner asked as she came up to her.

The girl quickly became startled, shutting the music box. He wanted her to go back to the way she had been a moment before.

When her tongue peeked out to lick her lips, he eagerly waited to hear the voice that belonged to her.

"Y-yes." She went back to looking at the box, avoiding the gaze of the woman. "H-how much is it?"

"Three thousand dollars."

She removed her fingers from the piece. "Oh."

The woman kindly smiled. "I know Christmas just passed, but you could always ask for it for your birthday, maybe. I could hold it."

She shook her head. "Thank you, but it's too much."

The lady smiled. "Well, you could always come back if you talk your parents into it."

"Thank you." The girl took one last glance at the music box before she left the store.

Watching her leave was harder than he had thought it would be. He wouldn't be able to come out of the store until she pulled out. Therefore, he had to watch her go to the car through the display window, and that wasn't close enough for him.

A vibration in his pocket had him pulling out his cell phone. He didn't say a word when he accepted the call.

His friend Sal came over the phone. "The BMW is registered to Maxwell Masters."

That wasn't what he had expected, though it explained why he felt like he had seen her before.

"Girl," Lucca spoke into the phone carefully, watching her approach the driver's side.

"He's married to Elaine Maste—"

"Younger," he cut him off.

Sal paused. "Scar?"

Lucca's eyes traced her markings. "Yes."

"That's Maxwell's daughter, Chloe Masters."

He ended the call with the push of a button.

Time stood still for him as he soaked in anything and everything he could about her before she disappeared into the car.

There was always a moment one faced in life when a choice had to be made, and this was his.

Her tortured soul called to his dark one, whispering for him to save her. His heart was now slow, steady, finding its purpose—*Chloe Masters* . . .

Taking one last look at the scar on her face, he couldn't wait for the day he could run his fingers across it. *Beautiful.*

THE BEING BEHIND THE DOOR

T he cold, metal table underneath her was a stark contrast to her burning face from what seemed like pointless crying.

"Please! Stop!" No amount of her kicking and fighting was a match for what felt like millions of hands holding her down.

The laughter from the evil man who held a knife rang through her ears, mocking.

"Stay still, little girl"—he drew the knife closer to her face—"or it'll just hurt worse."

Looking at his abnormally large, black eyes, she was sure she was looking into the eyes of the devil …

The silver blade inched closer and closer to her right eye until it was mere centimeters from her pupil.

"Don't blink."

A tear welled up in her eye, making it even harder as she struggled to keep her eye open. Her body began to tremble. She was going to blink.

"Don't blink, little girl," he warned her again.

The tear fell, and her eye started to close . . .

"Chloe!" Amo's voice boomed.

A flicker of light entered her mind.

"This way, Chloe!" Amo pleaded.

Another flicker of light had her eyes shooting open. Sitting up so abruptly made her feel lightheaded. The bed, along with the big room, was one she didn't recognize, which made her heart pound like a drum in her ears.

No! He's got me, and no one knows I'm even here.

Shakily, Chloe stood from the bed, going over to the nightstand. Her hand reached out . . .

The devil will kill me this time. He promised me he would.

Once she opened the expensive, gold music box, the familiar lullaby began to play. It was then she realized that it couldn't be hers. Chloe stepped to the huge window with a hitch in her breath. She slowly reached out to pull back the curtain.

No one will save me this time.

Pulling back the curtain, she held her breath as she was greeted with a beautiful garden along with the white gazebo she had found herself under before with . . .

The door creaked open, and Chloe turned to meet the being behind the door.

The dark voice made her gasp for air.

"Hey, darlin'."

THE MOMENT

Y*ou thought she had a* choice? No. The Boogieman had decided her fate the moment he had looked upon her scarred face.

THE MOMENT

There's *always a moment one* faces in life,
A moment one could never forget.
And in this moment, you would swear time stood still.

After that moment, the tears begin to burn your cheeks.
Your soul feels as if it were touched by darkness.
And even if you never believed in God, your knees begin to bleed from praying so much.

I faced that moment,
A moment I will never forget.
And in that moment, time did stand still.

But my cheeks healed with time.
My soul fought the darkness with light.
And my knees, now calloused and scarred, are stronger than ever for the next moment when time stutters.

Sarah Brianne

Please, if you or someone you know ever needs help,
follow this link to get more information and help.
YOU ARE NOT ALONE.

www.victimsofcrime.org/help-for-crime-victims
/national-hotlines-and-helpful-links